SAMUEL TAYLOR'S LAST NIGHT

Grateful acknowledgment is made to *absent magazine*, where a portion of chapter 1 appeared earlier.

Library of Congress Cataloging-in-Publication Data

Amato, Joe, 1955-
    Samuel Taylor's last night / Joe Amato. -- First Edition.

    pages cm
    ISBN 978-1-62897-099-9 (pbk. : alk. paper)
    1. Taylor, Samuel, 1912-2000--Fiction. I. Title.
    PS3551.M184S36 2014
    813'.54--dc23

                    2014010842

Partially funded by a grant by the Illinois Arts Council, a state agency

ILLINOIS
ARTS
COUNCIL
AGENCY

www.dalkeyarchive.com

Cover: design and composition by Mikhail Iliatov
Printed on permanent/durable acid-free paper

SAMUEL TAYLOR'S LAST NIGHT

Joe Amato

DALKEY ARCHIVE PRESS
Champaign / London / Dublin

for Kass

Some men a forward motion love,
But I by backward steps would move . . .

Henry Vaughan

CONTENTS

1   SAMUEL TAYLOR'S "LAST NIGHT"

A writer is someone who can make a riddle out of an answer.

Karl Kraus

Last night, talking with Iraq's Prime Minister, I confided in him that I was allergic to sand. He confided in me that he doubted the Shia would prevail. Together we improvised a serving of *Phoenix dactylifera* to be presented by a partisan of Ali to one of the surviving actors from a 1965 film about a plane crash in the Sahara. Ours would be a truly cinematic peace, as Lara Logan reported later on the CBS *Evening News.*

Last night a close Sunni friend confessed to me that she had no idea so many combat deaths in WWII were caused by flying pieces of shattered bone. I confessed to her that I had no idea the vast majority of the world's Muslims were followers of the caliphate. And imagine, I said, if you were allergic to sand. Imagine, she said—for every American killed during that war, 7 Japanese were killed, 17 Germans were killed, and 60 Russians were killed. Or something like that. Imagine, I said, if you were allergic to gluten. Imagine, she said, what it means when hell becomes just another place on the map, and the Baghdad of poets and pictures, whether west or east of the Tigris, becomes hell. That reminds me, I said, of what Richard Boone growls to Paul Newman near the end of a terrific 1967 western: "Now what do you suppose hell is gonna look like?"

Last night I found myself at a powwow north of Pocatello, Idaho, wondering why so many Mormons decided to settle here. It was a sunny day, unbearably hot and desert dry. There was a massacre of Shoshoni taking place midwinter an hour's drive to the southeast, while at the powwow, an eagle feather dropped from a dancer's costume, and time stood still for a moment. After the massacre, I found myself in downtown Pocatello, where everyone was dressed in Civil

War garb. My wife was there too, trying to pretend she didn't know me. She was hawking her first book, about a little-known massacre of Shoshoni, which, she'd concluded, was followed by a mass rape. "Look," I heard her say to one old man with a beard and a hair shirt, "this sort of thing is happening *today*." And when I heard her say that, I suddenly recalled that we were trying to option a screenplay about the massacre.

Last night consider, as Exhibit A, James Caan in a Howard Hawks western reciting lines from a poem by Edgar Allan Poe. Last night consider, as Exhibit B, Dino and Ricky singing together in what most of us regard as Hawks's original version. Last night I preferred the latter to the former, but Robert Mitchum was a hoot in the former.

Last night, dodging bullets, a man among men, I took great pleasure in all things Ruritanian.

Last night the expression on that dog's face. Don't tell me that motherfucker wasn't smiling.

Last night no algorithms, no litigants, no white paper, no feature creep, but composites abound. Last night someone persistently invoked *post hoc*, and we couldn't tell whether it was the persistence or the fallacy itself that brought about the end of true dialogue all over the world—a kind of hush, and one that had nothing to do with falling in love on Facebook. Last night, day for night, it did and it didn't add up.

Last night I was sitting Zazen in a bar in Riga—make that Rio—reading a book by Edward Said and enjoying a cold one, when a little boy, couldn't have been more than eight years old, asked me if I had a buck. You look like my kid, I said, if I'd had kids. I didn't tell him that his complexion was a shade darker than I imagined my kid's would have been if I'd had kids, but really—who gives a shit? I flipped him a fifty-cent piece, and the squirt ran off half-satisfied—all told, an experience not unlike those you see in films from the thirties and forties, and maybe even fifties, that depict Americans abroad acting like Americans. Except that I could just make out through the boy's tee a small pistol tucked into the back of his belt. Yep, I thought, that's my boy, and boys will be boys.

Last night I awoke in deep pain, having gone to bed too soon after eating too much pepperoni and sausage pizza. I got up, took a piss, and recollected a poem I'd written while working as an engineer in a pharmaceutical plant. It was an unabashedly lyrical item, written before I really knew what "lyrical" meant, having to do with Theodora of Byzantium, *Lepidoptera*, and my beloved Claude Achille, who while on his deathbed could hear the Germans bombing his beloved City of Light. Were they using Zeppelins at the time? I didn't think so. *La Mer* played softly in the background, transporting me to a discourse—and here I beg you to listen closely—in which the problem of the critical idiom was posed as having primarily to do not with knowledge production, but with knowledge *relations*. In which case, I could hear myself respond, why am I having such a difficult time relating? And then it dawned on me, even as the morning sky brightened—giving me pause to consider what it means for paper to reflect blue light with a wavelength of exactly 457 nanometers, 44 nanometers wide—that this had much to do with days long past. In particular, with those visits I would pay to my mother while she worked as the main receptionist at General Electric CR & D in Schenectady. I was pursuing a doctorate in English at the time. Across the lobby from my mother's desk sat Edison's desk, atop which burned a low-voltage, tungsten-filament, incandescent bulb that, as I recall, had been burning for many decades. If you walked through the reception area, it opened out to a veranda overlooking the Mohawk. I would sit in a chair beside my mother, and we'd chat for a half-hour in between her various duties. I learned some local institutional lore—the days of the deformed and brilliant Steinmetz, the mechanical horse once built there, contributions to the Big Bang Theory. One of the scientists gave me a copy of the *The Principle of Relativity*, with original papers by Einstein, Lorentz, Weyl, and Minkowski. "A DOVER EDITION DESIGNED FOR YEARS OF USE!" $1.75. It sits even now on our shelves. One bright August day, while I was visiting with my mother, the mailman dropped off a number of packages wrapped in twine, which my mother signed for. She looked at the twine, tsking gently, and retrieved a large pair of shears from her desk drawer, snipping the twine from the packages. She turned to the waist-high cabinet behind her, saying, without any particular emphasis, "I try to show them how much they waste." And as she said this, she reached down into the cabinet to pull out a ball of twine perhaps one foot in diameter, quickly wrapping the snipped twine around the ball and knotting it into the other snippets. "Jesus Christ, Mom!" I laughed, trying not to laugh too loudly. She smiled, still visibly annoyed at the "waste." "You should have seen the last ball I showed them—it was this big." She spread her hands apart to indicate two feet. A quick burp, and it was back to bed for another couple of hours of shuteye.

Last night, it occurred to me that, like many poets, I'm easily distracted by what's immediately before me. Last night, I couldn't get to sleep at all. No, no. And with the radio playing, or perhaps it was iTunes, I researched Woody "One Take" Van Dyke, intrigued by the man's fascinating and productive life—dying of cancer and suffering from heart problems, he committed suicide at the age of 53—and someone looking over my shoulder, who looked something like my younger self back when I had a perm and who had at that moment a particular yen for New York School antics, spotted a typed, aging letter in an old trunk stored in the attic of my dear friend and correspondent, Michael of New Hamburg, NY, who is of late an ami of Hélène's. Michael has some great stories to tell, and he told me that the undated document—evidently, to the best of Michael's reckoning, written by a mysterious man named after Lamont Cranston, whose alter ego, The Shadow, was created by Maxwell Grant, the pen name of the magician Walter B. Gibson, the author of 187 books— might well be understood as a precursor to our appetite for the virtual. Either that, or pure apocrypha. "Dear Soul," the letter began, "unless you're Gertrude Stein, and even then, writing about *now* has always been a tricky proposition, *now* becoming *then* even more quickly than might be suggested by the few millimeters separating the former bit of italic from the latter. *Now* is prior to *then* in the foregoing sentence, both materially and temporally, but then, as we all know, *then* often points to a prior state, even if every now and then we get a lay glimpse of the grammatical difficulty when talking about a (back) *then* during which something *then* transpired. There's the nominal *then*, that is, and then there's the adverbial *then*, which often refers to what comes next, right up until the thing coming next is now. And *then*—and *now*—and then again, no need to wax so metalinguistic. For the truth about *then* is that *then* is the body, and you, Dear Soul, are the *now*. Continually flanked by the body, it is all you can do to resist dissolution. And yet you persevere, and this is because, without you, the body cannot find its disparately moral bearings from one conscious moment to the next. Not consciousness, nor spirit, nor some complex of emotion and intellect, you, Dear Soul, tickle sentience into something properly called *being*—purposive being. When the body passes, you pass with it. But the body cannot pass, cannot transition without you." There was more, much more, the sort of thing you find in graduate theses that cite Continental theorists by way of presuming to punch holes in Continental theory—but I didn't have the heart to read the rest. I thought about her then, and what I'd gladly surrender to keep her now. The radio was still playing, or perhaps it was iTunes. And it occurred to me that I might be too clever by half. Me, a smart aleck—too thick, too recondite, too relational. Last night notwithstanding, nobody left off the hook.

Last night, it would begin, "In the pages that follow, everyone lives. Meaning, everyone dies. And, the woman at the stove makes sauce from made sauce. Allow us to explain: This morning, in her freezer, nestled between a four-pound loin roast and two packages of sweet sausage links—*salsiccia*, her grandparents would call it—sits a small glass container of sauce. The sauce contains sauce made from a small container of sauce stored previously in the freezer, which contains sauce made from a small container of sauce stored previously in the freezer, which contains—and so on, all the way back to the 4th of July, 1956. Family lore has it that, on this day, her Calabrian grandfather brought home to her Sicilian grandmother a used General Electric refrigerator, with a small freezer compartment. For the first time, Grandma Rotella could set aside a few cups of her sauce for use in future sauces, and by future generations. Call it a planned leftover—or, as all sauces begin with what some call a base, the ur-foundation. And as each generation would invariably tweak the family recipe a notch, preservation and improvisation would go hand-in-hand." There you have it: the ur-story-within-the-story—a lesson in reading. Now let it go, amico.

Last night at the Quick Lane to have new tires put on our Nissan pickup the service manager talks about how he killed cars during the Cash for Clunkers program way back during the early 21st century, before the flood. "We poured this liquid glass stuff—at least I call it that—into the crankcase with a coupla quarts of water, then revved the engine up to around 5000 rpm. The engines just froze right up, except for that 5 liter Mustang engine. Had to do it twice with that baby. Threw a rod and blew one radiator, but it wasn't very exciting after the first dozen or so vehicles. Killed eighty-six total. Some of those cars and vans and trucks were in perfect condition, so it was tough at times." We talk about the cars we drove when we first learned to drive—him, a 1962 F100, me, a 1960 DeSoto—and reminisced about the good old days at GM. The Rocket V8. The '69 Camaro. But in the final analysis, even the automotive world makes no sense, and last night, as the automotive world goes, so goes the world. Last night, notional atmospherics and a desire to avoid the past perfect.

Last night I was an investigative reporter, and I trailed a guy who looked an awful lot like Dr. Mabuse to 1600 Pennsylvania Ave. I don't think I need to tell you what happened next.

Last night the night is chilly, but not dark.

Last night bragging rights, followed by a feeling of elation, followed by slipping on a banana peel. Last night they were glomming onto my buckets of rain, confusing a good cry for a reason to cry. Last night crocodile tears, a hint of perfidy at the periphery, and a moral to our singsong story of God and man in the third tier.

Last night I was overcome by that same sense of dread I experienced as a kid upon first encountering Roger Corman's *Attack of the Crab Monsters*. Really. Thus overcome and seeking relief via hair of the dog, I tried through Netflix to get a hold of *The Vampire* (1957), starring John Beal, Colleen Gray, Kenneth Tobey, and Dabbs Greer. I was curious whether this little programmer had held up, and was hoping for at least a few of the shudders I felt over forty years ago. Netflix was a no-go, but I found it at Amazon's Video on Demand service ($1.99). It held up. And my sense of dread dissipated. Really.

Last night, while my wife's left foot was in a splint after surgery to remove two—which turned out to be three—bone chips, which procedure precipitated my sleeping on the couch for a week so that she might get in and out of bed with her crutches to pee without waking me, our new-ish couch making, in all, for a reasonably comfortable sleeping arrangement, God spoke to me. Or maybe it was the Devil. Or maybe it was some Victorian novelist's Fairy Godmother. Whoever the fuck it was, he assured me that you're not going to hell if you drive a little drunk, or if you don't buckle your seat belt, or if you throw your gum wrapper out the car window, or if you ride your bike without a helmet, or if you walk on the wrong side of the street, or if you eat a Big Mac, or if you smoke, or if you don't floss, or if you screw-over, or screw, a subordinate, or if you forget to take your vitamins, or if you don't lose any sleep over inmates on death row, or if you voted for Bush 43, or if you find yourself thinking racist thoughts, or if your sexual fantasies are a little twisted, or if you don't believe in God, or the Devil, or some Victorian novelist's Fairy Godmother—in which event you already *know* you're not going to hell—or if you're a dumbass, or if you'd rather follow than lead, or if you don't care how you look, or if you fart in public, or if you fart in public *and* fail to report it to the authorities, or if you don't close your mouth while you chew, or if you believe there's nothing you can do to make the world a better place, or if you forget to say the magic word, or if you're not a good neighbor, or if you hurt someone to stop them from hurting you, or if you choose not to reproduce, or if you're not entirely mature, or if you default on your student loan, or if you don't bring your car in for an oil change every 3000 goddamn miles, or if you don't do the laundry every week, or if you don't speak a second language or play the piano, or if you don't turn down the thermostat, or if you fail to show the proper respect, or if you don't buy USA, or if you don't save enough money, or if you experience road rage, or if the sum total of your creative output amounts to recycling the myths of your generation, or even if you feel the urge every now and then to kick the shit out of someone who's behaving like an asshole. "But rest assured," added God or the Devil or some Victorian novelist's Fairy Godmother, "you *are* going to hell if you don't tip well. So ante up, skinflint, ante up."

Last night the whole purpose of art was to elicit sympathy for those who have no purpose. Last night was this mumblecore, or what?

Last night how is it that when I'm sitting in our living room of late and talking with my wife we've taken to referring to a despicable woman as a *cunt* without batting an ironic eye but would never ever refer to a despicable African American as a *nigger* without a very, very carefully managed irony? And was it OK if we sang along with Patti Smith's "Rock 'n Roll Nigger"? And was I using the n-word in my writing simply to give it some punch, in which event—. Last night, cause for concern? But last night, deracination was not an option, especially not with an ethnic <rotfl> surname.

Last night I loved the anger in Pete Townshend's voice, and the play-fulness in Bing's, and the confidence in Sinatra's. Last night, *aller guten Dinge sind drei.*

Last night, did you think Louis Armstrong ever hit a wrong note?

Last night fuck constraints—a mansion for me.

Last night, I translated into English some recent prose in English by

K. I showed the translation to K, and he told me to go back to the drawing board. I told him I'd left my drawing board in the darkness, where, if B were correct, I figured I could still sing *about* the darkness. He told me that the darkness was more sinister than I'd imagined, and might overwhelm B and me both. I wondered whether, just to be fair, I should substitute "light" for "darkness" whenever I rehearsed this tale, if only to correct the same old metaphorical and racialized imbalance. This despite the fact that an absence of light has always frightened me more than an abundance. This despite the fact that it does little good to try to teach anyone anything if your very presence evokes a nurse in a burn ward, or a sap. This despite the fact that C's get degrees, beers get careers. This despite the fact that John Q. Public will never regard fragments as on a par with wholes, no matter how fragmented John Q's grasp of reality. This despite the fact that mortgage rates are at an all-time sigh. I went back to the drawing board, at any rate, and designed a better trope, one that wouldn't buckle under too much utopia. The unresolved question of an overriding telos left me with a bad taste in my mouth for days afterward, but we yet felt incredibly aroused whenever they substituted "we" for "I" and "they" for "you" during sex. Pass me a shandy, Mesopotamia, we've got the blues on the run, Rumi, so let me hear your freelance balalaikas ringing out *Zang tumb tuum*, O whirling text-massaged world.

Last night, my trainer explained to me how to exercise my right shoulder if I hoped to recover quickly from what's known these days as a *rotator cuff injury*. I'd initially injured the shoulder working out, and really put the screws to it six days later shoveling snow for two hours during a blizzard. That Central Illinois wind is a bitch, let me tell you. Actually, I think the shoulder was about to go anyway, as I've injured it a few times over the course of my life—pegging a ball five or six times to my wife, for instance, a couple of years back—and have never really done what I should to get it back in shape. More pushups, for one. It's my right shoulder, and I'm right-handed, which, I've learned, is typical. I shovel (and sweep) left-handed, however. I think this is because my father was a southpaw, though here again, he wrote right-handed. Blame it on the nuns, he would say. In fact, I think I will. It's the nuns who did this to my shoulder. It's the motherfucking nuns. And I know now what it means to present grotesque caricatures of occupation or ethnicity or social class as a means of undercutting the persistence of such caricatures. Pursued diligently and with careful attention to the ironies at stake, it's certainly possible to do positive cultural work by contrasting such caricatures with the prejudicial belief systems that give rise to them. It's certainly possible. But what was more on my mind was whether I'd become an old guy with a bum soldier. I mean, shoulder.

Last night it wasn't my bag. Last night I was fly, hardcore, rowdy as all get-out. Last night I was dialed-in like nobody's business, the ubiquitous You of YouTube, said the working-class Italian-Alsatian hiker in me. Last night Fred, my paisan, voiced his consent. Last night that's good enough for me.

Last night, like the night before, and like tonight, and like tomorrow night, I'm reading *A Bright Shining Lie: John Paul Vann and America in Vietnam*. I'm thinking, this is a long book. I'm thinking, it's the right time in my life to be reading such a long book. I'm thinking, I don't think I'll ever manage to write such a long book.

Last night Raymond Shaw is the kindest, bravest, warmest, most wonderful human being I've ever known in my life. Last night and dig that score by David Amram.

Last night bear scat on the trail, we proceed on the *qui vive*, fretting the durée of Empire and impending appropriations of all that heaven allows.

Last night was all about *content*, both as a noun and as an adjective. Tomorrow night promises a lexical encounter with the word *amplexus*. Tonight we were struck by Mark Shield's claim that there's been a "coarsening" of the public domain, and we ask ourselves whether our proclivity for four-letter words has had unanticipated effects, contributing to a lapse of civil behavior among the fucking jerks on this parlous Anthropocenic orb.

Last night racial profiling seemed insidious, but not as insidious as pretending that once a crime has been committed, or if a threat to public safety appears imminent, we will not endeavor to profile the criminal. Last night the FBI profiler, a tall-ish black guy in a suit and tie and sporting sunglasses, concurred.

Last night a fennel seed from a sausage link I'd eaten twelve hours prior came dislodged, and biting into it I was reminded of how far I'd come, and how far I had left to go.

Last night since when does *balanced* mean that for every sound proposition we needs must entertain its cockeyed counterpart? That's the hallmark of the unbalanced, unless of course you're one of those jokers who believe that evolutionary theory is merely a conjecture. We'll get back to this another day.

Last night, what's more important: trying to do exceptionally well what everyone else does, or doing what I and I alone can do?

Last night I was gay. No—straight. No.

Last night my Oz friend and correspondent, Maryanne, who was visiting family in Pakistan, sent me the following from an Islamabad (pop. 800,000) newspaper: "29,646 vehicles challaned [fined] in Sept." The breakdown: 690 - using cell phones; 171 – under age; 759 – overloading (private transport); 1,584 – violating traffic signals; 911 – public transport vehicles impounded; 39 – overspeeding; 3,371 – overloading (public transport); 1,004 – no headlights; 1,985 – wrong side of the road; 5,352 - zebra crossings; 1,366 – creating hurdles in the smooth flow of traffic; 313 – reckless driving; 1,141 – using compression horns; 157 – emitting smoke; 107 – no fitness certificate; 2,471 – for not using helmets when driving the motorcycles [*sic*].

Last night, "so I'm sitting on the couch with Tomato #1, having a discussion with her that will invariably lead to a stormy breakup, when the phone rings. I don't have caller ID at this time, so I pick it up. It's Tomato #2 calling, as I knew she would eventually, not to apologize for the wretched behavior that led to our stormy breakup, but to secure from me some kind of assurance that I didn't wish her soul to suffer everlasting damnation. So I alert Tomato #2 to the fact that Tomato #1 is on the line, Tomato #2 having been apprised of the whole sordid little story, and Tomato #2 proceeds to scribble on a pad what I should say to Tomato #1. Needless to say, juggling Tomatoes of this caliber is not without its dialogical difficulties. As a result of which, I end up afterward troubled by the thought that I've been less than generous to Tomato #1. But that thought soon passes as I become embroiled in Tomato #2's passive-aggressive antics, the corollary of a near-pathological guardedness that, in its capacity for wreaking psychological damage, far exceeds Tomato #1's emotional immaturity. Why was I so drawn to Tomatoes, you may well ask? Ah, but that's the beauty of Tomatoes—to draw within their orbits those who have developed a taste for pulp."

Last night, like last year, in whatever direction I turned, there was Mark McGurl, at a slightly higher elevation, charting the cosmological ebbs and flows, showing beyond a shadow of a doubt how my work as a writer, however raggedyass it may be, nonetheless served as testament to that great workshop in the sky out of which cosmology itself had tumbled. Last night, like last year—what a conceit.

Last night, at dinner with a group of her fellow academics, one of them spilled a glass of water all over himself, explaining, sheepishly, "It was a positive meniscus." When the check came, she asked, boisterously, "What's the damage?" But everyone went about their business, each scholar carefully adding up his or her portion of the bill, in the process neglecting the tip. Which she picked up. An ordinary evening in New Haven, last night, the plainness of plain things.

Last night, the subject was the object, and the object was a subject, and the subject was no longer living. Last night, what ghostlier agencies?

Last night, to return to a prior topos, or Post-it®, my brother Mike and I were good and pissed off when the cops stopped us at a sobriety checkpoint at three in the a.m. Eastern Standard Time in the village of Liverpool for no obvious reason other than that we were out at three in the a.m. Eastern Standard Time in the village of Liverpool driving a 1975 Toyota Corolla E5, and our anger was perhaps akin to Henry Louis Gates, Jr.'s when they rousted him out of his home in Cambridge, Mass., because he was a black man in a big house. Last night racial profiling was wrong if it meant that people of color and of the underclasses would be treated as more likely to be guilty of something, but racial profiling was OK if it meant that intelligence agencies would attempt to profile terrorists here and abroad. Last night the notion that little old ladies from Atlanta or Des Moines would be treated at airport checkpoints in the same way as able-bodied men like myself seemed a positively absurd response to equality under the law, as did the suspension of habeas corpus for the prisoners at Gitmo. Last night a South Carolina congressman shouted "You lie!" to the first African-American President of the United States during a presidential address on health care to a joint session of Congress. Last night, whatever else, racism was in the cards. Last night was a complicated affair.

Last night I was awakened from a deep slumber by a booming tenor who was on his way to becoming a booming baritone. "We have two things to worry about," the voice intoned, imperiously, "people who blow themselves up to make a point, and people who think they're making perfect sense when they attempt to draw a hard and fast distinction between the intentional killing of civilians and the dropping of bombs on populated areas with the express purpose of killing only enemy combatants." But at what point is reckless endangerment of civilians equivalent to premeditated murder, I whispered, half awake? "See, for instance, New York Penal Law 120.25, revised 15 June 2006," the voice advised, "which includes the clause, 'under circumstances evincing a depraved indifference to human life.'" But this isn't a matter of law enforcement, I protested—and the voice fell silent, calling my bluff. In fact the word "depraved" *had* caught me off-guard, moving me at once beyond the relative complacency of war-is-hell truisms and my own sleepy discourse. Depraved. Godammitall to hell, I thought. Last night, half-awake, I caught a glimpse of myself as others see me: just another poor bastard who thinks his life is worth a permanent entry in the archive, a few vital memories, and a scarifying truckload of fuck yous. So why the heavy weather? Mud swirled in gradients of longing, sweet ache of age, a failure of the elements, the signature of distant orbits in the dead of night—it was a climate of loss ennobling in its destruction: for a few precious moments, George Sanders would have been proud of me, especially with that halo over his head.

Last night, while gazing at your tattoo, I gradually realized just how full of shit you are when you use the word *diversity*.

Last night maybe I was wrong. Maybe *Carrie* wouldn't have been a better movie if it weren't a horror story. And maybe if you make a film about 1970 it doesn't have to have the feel and look of a film *made* in 1970. And maybe what we need is not less, but *more* stimulation. And maybe, last night, I was right.

Last night, if you're in a street fight and outnumbered, you can kick your opponents in the balls, yes? Accordingly, we ought to grant Michael Moore, whatever his sins of omission, some corresponding leeway. So sayeth the belching stomach of Syracuse, present and accounted for.

Last night I did a perfect impression of Frank Gorshin doing Kevin Spacey. Last night Orientalisms left me in the lurch? Or was it simply multitasking? Last night he was better when he was low budget? Last night more URLs hosting porn or soi-disant trivia. Last night a spoof of life at the server farm, expending vast amounts of energy. Last night you'll have to do better than that. Last night could this be Malta?

Last night my literal-minded students caught things that I, in my figurative-minded zeal, had missed. Last night the prereq for this semester's Intro to Creative Writing course would be Fact vs. Truth 101. Teaching evaluations would be out of the question. Last night the meat industry and its sordid practices were turning *me*, a lifelong devotee of porterhouse and pork chop, into a vegetarian. Last night the field was lodged. Last night she was worried about B.O.—that's box office, crew. Last night where was I?

Last night your type went out of style, and you couldn't buy a new one. Last night a silk scarf checkered in orange, brown and white with the name "Vera" on it. Last night was it your checkered past that surfaced, or the passing of things that were supposed to have lasted, that should have lasted? Last night Milankovitch cycles at Nomadics, and 3D in your living room. Last night dated you, and like all last nights, a record of barbarism, but no exit strategy.

Last night, in anticipation of how you might respond to my prompts, I tried to be more lucid, and was greeted by utter silence.

Last night was a lark. I dreamed I liked to write, like, [Product placement] poetry, because I was, like, a [Product placement] poet, who wrote, like, [Product placement] poems. I liked, like, similes, and liked to use at least, like, three per poem. I liked *like* more than *as*, like a guy who likes, like, [Product placement] tuna on, like, [Product placement] rye more than [Product placement] wheat. Or, like, crunchy more than smooth [Product placement]. It's a matter of, like, taste, and like they say, there's no accounting for, like, taste, especially, like, bourgeois taste. I should know, as they say. I awoke convinced that I simply must start my own [Product placement] political podcast, and find a way to keep the dumbfucks at bay, *pace* Rod Serling. Either that, or sing a [Product placement] hymn, unencumbered by [Product placement] branding. Later that night, a series of recollections led to a fortune inside a fortune cookie from Thai House in Bloomington, IL. The fortune was accompanied by a fortune that read, "Your dreams reveal important truths." This was winter 2007.

She got the same fortune, and had the same dream. Perhaps it was the food, but we weren't about to stop and discuss it, not with that much bread in our pockets. And no—were a penny dropped from the top of the Empire State Building to land on your head, it wouldn't kill you. And it wouldn't kill you to drop by now and then, genius.

Last night, under Caesar's watchful eye and with the exuberant Colosseum crowd cheering him on—only moments after a drug commercial for erectile dysfunction and with an activist court in session and a year prior to having learned that a woman had lost her balance and stumbled into a Picasso at the Metropolitan Museum of Art (this was after de Montebello's tenure as director, but before the new *Spartacus* series on Starz)—underdog Anthony Quinn defeated and put a sword to the throat of charioteer Jack Palance, Palance playing the villain with great gusto and Quinn putting in a solid turn as the spiritually tormented protagonist of the film's title, Barabbas. Five years earlier, Palance had played the lead in Rod Serling's teleplay, *Requiem for a Heavyweight*, and at nearly the same time *Barabbas* was released, Quinn could be viewed as the lead in the film version of *Requiem*. And some years prior, Palance had been an understudy both to Quinn and to Marlon Brando for the role of Stanley Kowalski. Quinn won two Best Supporting Actor Oscars, Palance won one, though his came much later in life, when Palance was 73. Both men liked to paint, though Quinn was probably the more accomplished visual artist. Physically, Palance was the fitter of the two. Palance died at the age of 87 in 2006, Quinn at the age of 86 in 2001. I suppose it all comes out in the wash.

Last night, like the night before, I was struck by how vital it is to set aside some time to examine the conditions under which one has come to desire what one has come to desire. It seemed incumbent upon me, as it had the night before—at the risk, then, of appearing twice ungrateful—to hold my institutional surrounds at arm's length, as it were, so as to inspect them thoroughly and without mercy. I began to understand, as I had the night before, how much I owed to realities that were by their very nature unjust. And for some strange reason, I recalled then, as I had the night before, what Rod Serling said about "never mak[ing] the mistake of assuming the audience is any less intelligent than you are."

Last night, while contemplating how a tragic turn of events can catch one unawares, I fancied myself a widower, and was struck by the sense of profound guilt I experienced at the mere thought of liberation from the constraints of marital bliss. Guilt, because despite the unfathomable loss, I was aroused at the prospect of that newfound eroticism which emerges from those carefully manicured distances shared by casual intimates. I knew my wife would understand, having fancied herself a widow more times than she might care to admit. My wife, my one wife, my one and only. I'm her second husband, and we both come from broken homes, and we suspect this has something to do with why we're still together. Along with the absence of a Vronsky, or a Madame Olenska. Oh and we both watch our carbs.

Last night when did I start saying "my trainer"? Last night 30 grams of fiber. Last night nasal irrigation. Last night my vitamins and minerals and a foam roller for my sore iliotibial band. Last night the evangelist. Last night the eager autodidact. Last night panned and scanned. Last night psychedelic was *in*, like xeriscaping and lifestyles and Flynn. Make that Flint. No—make that Walter Mitty.

Last night night harvesting. Last night could this be Mongibeddu?

Last night green figs, yoghurt, coffee, very black.

Last night OK let's settle this like men but first let me change my tampon.

Last night she smiles me into meaning, and stars fracture 'Bama.

Last night, in mourning: another author has killed off the wife.

Last night I bet five bucks to a dollar that Henry Adams had never heard of the "virgin cure." Tragically, I argued, too many men on the African continent and elsewhere *have* heard of it. This got me to ranting about tolerance, and I launched into a little diatribe about how once it absorbs its opposite, intolerance, it's not an especially useful notion, anymore than is democracy. For some reason my rant brought to one listener's mind the famed 11th edition of the *Encyclopædia Britannica*, "a marvelous mess of information," she said, "some of it far off the mark and highly offensive." She wondered what people a century hence would make of our achievements, our myths. Another listener asked whether any of us thought Doppler weather radar would still be around then. I wondered myself whether anyone would still be listening to "Green River" and whether "groovy" would still be, well, *groovy*. Last night, there would be no quibbling over vocations and avocations, our professions would cease to be the source of any real joy, our readers would claim to have found our voices and hung them out to dry, and we would be reproached presently for our stubborn refusal to abandon that outworn refrain of individuation, *ethos*. For whether consensus or dissensus prevailed, it was observed that our faith in the agency of the collective was predicated on our belief in human goodness, empathy, and volition, which might help to explain why we'd remained resolutely imperturbable despite our acknowledged failings of gene and genius, our lack of guts. And just as the omniscient voice seemed poised for a comeback, I overheard someone who sounded like Spencer Tracy say to someone who looked like Burt Lancaster, "Herr Janning, it 'came to that' the *first time* you sentenced a man to death you *knew* to be innocent."

Last night you, my friend, had that thing happen to you where you think you have a memory of a traumatic event, but it turns out that it couldn't possibly be your memory, so it must be your father's or your mother's memory—something akin to what Marianne Hirsch calls *postmemory*. Or perhaps it was the fuzzy memory you have of when you're a child imagining what your parents might have been remembering in the face of something horrible. Or perhaps any attempt to assess last night's performative process must be understood as a species of what economists call *survivorship bias*, an incomplete account emphasizing only those performance residues that have survived into the present. You couldn't describe the phenomenon to me, in any case, because you spoke only Hebrew, and I spoke only broken English, which left open the question of how I knew about your memories, down to the tiniest detail, and which question continued to haunt us throughout our deliberations. We both worried, too, about our shared inability to translate from and to our respective mother tongues, but we comforted each other in private by hugging each other and saying "Stephen King" three times, by way of indicating that Stephen King probably wasn't much of a translator, either. At the mere thought of Stephen King, however, we both remembered that there had been a traumatic event, and we decided then and there that it would be best for both parties if we ended our deliberations asap. Goodbye, my dear friend Godard, goodbye.

Last night I showed up for my country, but my country failed to show up for me.

Last night I learned that someone had stolen my identity, although frankly I was less worried about that than the possibility that someone might bulldoze the fields I played in as a kid.

Last night a small footprint, innocence yielding to experience. Last night, getting satori. Last night I developed a renewed appreciation for ball-peen hammers, if not AR-15s.

Last night I could see things with absolute clarity, things as they actually are: frat boys really *have* invaded the highest reaches of the US government, they really *don't* make jeans like they used to, unbridled corporate power really *is* destroying the planet, Americans really *are* obese, the gap between rich and poor really *is* intolerable, gun control and campaign finance reform really *do* matter, there really *is* such a thing as too much government and too little government, the color line and patriarchal power really *do* persist into the 21st century, and everything in general is about ten times more fucked up than our media outlets are letting on. On the positive side of the ledger, there really *is* life on other planets, King Shit *can't* rule over anything but a kingdom of shit, you *can* be dead wrong and still have a point, melody and rhythm and color and sentiment really *aren't* evil, and Olson was right—the will to change *does not* change. High time, I reckoned, to run for public office. That all is subjectively human does not obviate the need to take a stand, says he. Says he, to hazard a best guess. And a better guess. And so on. Because some things, he says, are given, whatever we make of them. And no—were a penny dropped from the top of the Empire State Building to land smack on your head, says he, it wouldn't kill you.

Last night we were all robots, busy devising a modified Turing Test to determine which of us still harbored the undesirable behavioral traits of our cyborg and human predecessors. Those who failed the test would be sent to the reconditioning clinic. We were as unsettled in the face of a deathless future as humans once were in the face of death, and thus wanted to prepare our populations for a stress-free forever-and-a-day. But it occurred to us last night that perhaps the inability to be content with one's lot was itself a human trait.

Last night, goodness, I can just make out "The Happy Farmer" playing in the background. Piano. Opus 68, No. 10. But last night, in truth, I wanted to hear "You're the Top" performed by William Gaxton and Dolores Grey on *The Ed Sullivan Show*, 24 February 1952.

Last night he tore his ACL, then his dog tore his ACL. Cost him two grand for surgery to repair his dog's torn ACL. Last night a dog's life, last night what the fuck.

Last night not "Dear God," but "God dear." Last night no angel, read it and weep.

Last night I wanted to schmooze with them, but they each had an asskisser superglued to their asses.

Last night I slid down the tongue-in-groove hallway in my knit slippers, and picked up a huge sliver in my right foot. A stranger was watching my antics and knew I would pick up the sliver, but opted not to warn me. I ended up with two infections in that wound and two trips to the emergency hospital, and after limping around for a period of eight months, I put on thirty pounds. I was a fat kid for five years, only stripping off the extra weight after playing baseball every day during the summer between my freshman and sophomore years in high school. My homeroom teacher didn't even recognize me. Wait a minute—I'm mixing up the film I saw again last night, one of the great films, with something that happened to me when I was eight years old. Nobody was watching me slide down that hallway. It's possible that what happened in a classroom some years ago is contributing to the confusion. It was the first class of the fall semester, and as I stood under the bright fluorescent lights reading the riot act to my students, I absentmindedly noticed a small cockroach crawling around on the floor near one male student's foot. I kept talking, at once aware of my audience but removed enough from the task at hand to glance down every now and then to check on the bug's progress. As I continued my excursion through the course requirements, the critter climbed atop the student's shoe. To this day I can't explain why, but I did nothing to let the kid know about the bug, not wanting perhaps to embarrass a student whose name I had yet to learn, but also—and here I can't be certain—not feeling predisposed to interrupt my little lecture by making a big deal out of a bug. Or perhaps I was curious as to what would happen next, though this implies an emotional distance that I can't account for, and which clearly cannot be justified. Anyway, after crawling around on the student's foot for a half a minute, the roach disappeared up the kid's pant leg. I concluded my lecture, and dismissed the class. And that, Dear Reader, is about as close as I come to K.

Last night, when the last search engine and find function and correlation machine and data mining device had excavated the last of human history and drawn what conclusions could be drawn, the specter of universality raised anxieties among intellectuals the world over, and there were reports of a celestial apparition whose majestic features were said to evoke an intelligence founded neither on deep knowledge nor on cheap capital, but on acquiescence to a vast Hegelian spirit that would suspend all quiddities in the name of the Same.

Last night Paul Krugman said "I told you so" and they gave me a Nobel Prize just for listening to the guy.

Last night I was hell-bent on writing the autobiographical campus novel the very existence of which registers one's triumph even as it documents the variously pedigreed forces that have brought about one's failure. Last night reflection itself was reflexive, as well it should be, author and narrator and character making laughing stocks of one another.

Last night, revanchist pleasure regnant, with regrets. And then she intimated, waggishly, that her medieval imaginary trumped my faux-*zuihitsu* couture any day.

Last night, did you really mean to write *couture*?

Last night, I really meant to write approximately what you're reading.

Last night the jar of Peter Pan peanut butter that my brother keeps in his garage—which he insists on hanging onto on questionable grounds, to wit: that it made him sick to his stomach and its lot number matches that of the nationally reported salmonella-contaminated containers—exploded for reasons unknown, and a team of newshounds appeared on the scene wanting to know whether the risk associated with keeping such a jar had been appropriately *tranched*. Mike and I shrugged our shoulders, donned our protective clothing, and went back to cleaning up the mess. Last night I'd been thinking way, way too much about the economy, to the point at which even a term like *partial derivative* was becoming difficult for me, a former math major, to parse without thinking of CDOs and the like. Last night peanut butter had become a metaphor for risk, risk had become a metaphor for corruption, corruption had become a metaphor for life, and I felt the earth shift as it turned harmless and stainless on its axis.

Last night, but what about churnalism?

Last night, back at the ranch, the full moon started out low on the horizon, that strangely reassuring off-yellow hue you see once in a blue moon. I was kneeling beside my bed, praying for the day when authors would stop writing once they ran out of things to say. I was kneeling at your feet, begging you not to use Botox to remove those beautiful furrows in your brow. I was down on my luck and on all fours, ambivalent about my youthful indiscretions, my indiscriminate use of words like "sacred" and "gypsy" and "Magic Marker"—as in "sacred gypsy Magic Marker"—entirely lacking the more sensible apprehension that a trap door might open at one's feet at any time, plunging one into a pool of Johnny Weissmuller-worthy crocodiles. I was boxing the compass, trying to get a handle on what the next best direction might be for a bloke who isn't afraid to enter the ring with one hand tied behind his back. I was tying one hand behind your back, pleading with you not to enter the ring with that large, buff shepherd who has a thing for espionage. I was in a Dalton Trumbo script, eating a hot dog with mustard near a fountain named after Dalton Trumbo, picturing myself a thousand miles and a world of humiliation away, where as lord of what little I surveyed, I would long for an end to all dislocations that are not self-imposed, and resolve to eliminate the term "wishful thinking" from my vocabulary.

Last night I had a daughter named Kass.

Last night in the year of our Lord one thousand nine hundred and seventy-six, all work had equal dignity. Last night we believed in higher callings. Last night we had convictions—crunchy convictions steeped in tradition and reeking of terroir. Last night, nothing in escrow, all options deselected, we were privy to the huffing and puffing of ontological atavism.

Last night "Would you care to join us?" was an act of exclusion.

Last night the Bossa Nova then nightnight *boa noite.*

Last night tomato blight. (A rhyme.) Last night I pissed off shit stains. Last night love was not the answer—bleach was. Last night favoritism still rankled, H1N1 was a distant memory, and I found myself quite alone in the heartland, crickets chirping extravagantly, the relationship between single-crop agribiz and one's sense of loyalty awaiting extensive cognitive deliberation.

Last night Funks Grove, the smell of fresh-baked pizza, Dickens and Beckett wagging their tails, the three of us chatting around the swing, pistachio shells covering the ground, and John, that dirty bastard, busting my chops for the umpteenth time. It was all too incestuous, according to *The Pantagraph.* Later, as my wife and I are leaving, the Milky Way.

Last night I was walking through the pharmaceutical plant in a pair of new shoes, on my way back to my office after having inspected a job site, when I accidentally stepped into a pool of—I think it might have been methyl isobutyl ketone, but I can't be certain. (I've written about this elsewhere, but at the time, I was mired in abstractions.) When I got home later that evening, I took off my shoes and placed them near the door, as I always do, and the next morning, my entire apartment smelled like the soles of my shoes. The odor was pungent, and nauseating. I tried everything—scrubbing the soles, soaking them in laundry detergent. No go. Finally, I took the shoes outside, doused the bottoms with lighter fluid, and lit them on fire. I let them burn for a minute or two, until the bottoms of the tan Vibram soles were charred black. The smell was gone, and the charring wasn't visible from the sides. Success. Eventually I gave the shoes to my father, whose triple-E foot gradually expanded the leather uppers to the point of bursting. He liked them well enough, but he was right—they didn't have enough arch support, enough bounce. In spite of which, today I own another pair of the same brand of shoes—the last pair I'll ever own, the pair I owned when, a little boozy, I jumped up on a locked gate one night in Lincoln Park, Chicago, having just left a chichi engagement party with my friend Andy, and landed a bit too hard as I vaulted to the sidewalk on the other side, damaging my left inside heel because of that lack of bounce. And because of the booze. Regardless, I attend assiduously to these shoes, as I attend to all of my shoes. It's almost as if I want these shoes to last *forever*, one's shoes having taken one, after all, to wherever one has gone.

Last night I read, "The three influenza pandemics of the 20th century shared a similar theme. In each outbreak approximately 30% of the population developed severe illness and approximately half of those ill individuals sought medical care" (Jeffrey R. Ryan, *Pandemic Influenza: Emergency Planning and Community Preparedness*, CRC Press, 2009). Holy Moly, I thought, caught in the midst of the H1N1 pandemic, and then recalled that I had read someplace that Homer had used the word "moly" in book 10 of *The Odyssey*: "He bent down glittering for the magic plant / and pulled it up / black root and milky flower— / a *molü* in the language of the gods—" (trans. Robert Fitzgerald). A quick trip to Wiktionary confirmed that it had been the source of my recollection, and further indicated that the first use of the euphemistic "Holy Moly" occurred in the Captain Marvel comic books of the early forties. As to "moly," there is "evidence to support the hypothesis that 'moly' might have been the snowdrop, *Galanthus nivalis*, which contains galanthamine, a centrally acting anticholinesterase" (Plaitakis A, Duvoisin RC, *Clinical Neuropharmacology* 6.1 (Mar. 1983): 1-5). Moreover, according to Wikipedia, anticholinesterase is also known as an acetylcholinesterase inhibitor, and occurs naturally as a venom or poison, is used in the production of nerve gas and to treat Alzheimers's, and can serve as an antidote to anticholinergic poisoning. Last night, imagine my surprise, while recovering from Swine, at seeing my exclamation of surprise lead me, ace researcher that I'd fleetingly become, full circle back to medical discourse. Shazam!

Last night I was in Southeast Asia observing other well-heeled travelers who, like me, would refuse to admit to themselves that they had traveled there believing they could revisit the past, intent on bringing back home with them a sense of redemption.

Last night what was it about feet and their figurations?

Last night lyricism fell hard on the heels of pulp fiction.

Last night I read about six states that banned tipping in the first decades of the twentieth century.

Last night—"Errors have been made. Others will be blamed." You were ebullient as we sat in the dark crunching popcorn together while the hero of *Quantum Entanglement v. Speed of Gravity* unraveled the cause of her own death.

"Last night, Ebola? Last night, no."

Last night Pierre Boulez was talking about having to have the requisite "tools" to be "original." I think he might have been right, kid.

Last night I was anxious about my appearance at the shop this morning, having been plagued by the apprehension that altogether too much emphasis is placed on what goes on there, pedagogically speaking. I'd been reading Paul Goodman, of course, while taking a break from the atelier. This was followed by a conversation in bed with my current thirty-something mistress—a curvy Rosario Dawson lookalike with a penchant for giving and receiving rim jobs—in which we discussed Joe Cocker's capacity for covering a song with such soulful brio as to make you forget it's a cover. Ms. thirty-something and I speculated together about what he might be like in person—I wanted to talk with him about the sixties and *Island of Lost Souls*, she wanted to fuck him big time while he sang to her, with me singing backup harmony—but my wife knocked on the door, so we called it a day, and returned to our regularly scheduled fantasies.

Last night was filled with compressed air and pneumatic lines and Shrader fittings and a noisy but durable single-cylinder air compressor mounted to a couple of old but sturdy planks connected via pulley and belt to an ancient but reliable electric motor mounted to the same planks and a copper pipe leading from said compressor to a weathered tank with pressure gauge and pop-off valve set at 80 psi and a young man growing old by the minute inhaling clouds of spray fumes and cigarette smoke and this apparatus and the young-man-growing-old-by-the-minute whose livelihood was tethered to it whose dreams were tethered to it whose mortal coil was tethered to it made and makes me want to tell the woman I love that the nature of my love will not will not will never permit this young man's lost opportunities to become mine, and by becoming mine, become hers. He taught me how to spell "naphtha."

Last night my brother and I were standing outside of the Westhill Cinema in Syracuse, NY, in a line of a hundred plus people, waiting to get in to see *Jeremiah Johnson*, a much-underrated film even today. It was snowing, the wind was howling, it was colder than a witch's cootchie. We'd heard on WNDR that the first 300 people to show up would get in free, and so there we were. And after a half-hour or so, everyone in the line was laughing and shivering, joking with one another that they hadn't bargained for this degree of foolishness. A community of the moment. We got in free all right, and freezing our butts off turned out to be just the right prelude to the film, with its many scenes of alpine expanse. The theater never got close to filling up, however, and by the time the house lights dimmed and the projector flickered, management was, wisely, letting everyone in free. Still, secretly we felt superior to the latecomers—like Jeremiah, and like Redford playing Jeremiah, and like Frank Silvera, and like Vladimir Sokoloff, and like Lila Kedrova, and like Martha Gellhorn, and like that kid in the wheelchair my brother spotted at an unforgettable George Carlin performance circa 1978 in downtown Syracuse—my brother spotted him just as we were busting out laughing at Carlin's routine about people with handicaps, our laughter transformed at once into mutual winces—we'd paid *our* dues, goddammit.

Last night I was watching a movie on network TV that had a lot to say about TV, much of it implicitly critical, and I found myself wondering whether I was watching a movie or watching TV, whether I was wallowing in the tacit assumptions of auteur theory or giving myself over to the ebbs and flows of the televised. Last night, was I engaged in meaningful provocation, or was I merely enjoying life? Last night, who was at the helm?

Last night I said to myself, *His work will still be read a hundred years from now. If I have anything to say about it.*

Last night she heard *anima*, while I heard *enema*. Is it possible we were both right?

Last night I wished mighty artists would be mighty human beings, and I wished mighty human beings would take time out to wish upon a star.

Last night the impossible aesthetics of *Beach Blanket Bingo* were, for an instant, completely justified.

Last night Nora said we were waiting for lightning to strike, so I grabbed a large flat-edge screwdriver that had belonged to my father and ran outside under virga waving it around above my head, while Nora stayed inside to work on her core. She'd fractured her left foot/ankle after a bad fall two months prior, and had to have surgery to remove two—which turned out to be three—bone chips, remember?—and I recall saying then that maybe this was an accident from which we could both learn. There are accidents and there are accidents, there are fractures and there are fractures, and there, in that diorama, are the Ancestral Rocky Mountains.

Last night I finally decided to get rid of my quarter-century old *American Heritage Dictionary* and crack open my unused 4th edition, which has sat on my shelf wrapped in plastic for some years now. Knowing that my mother had the Old World habit of inserting four-leaf clovers in all dictionaries, I was determined to extract any clovers prior to donating the volume. I recalled having seen a clover in the L's someplace, and flipping open the dictionary to that section, found one at "luck." But where might she have inserted others? I commenced to thumbing through every page of the dictionary, and found but one more clover, resting atop "die" on the recto. A premonition on her part? A poetic gesture, *coup de des* taken to its accidental limit? (She was, after all, French by birth.) And on that same recto, no less, "difference." But lo!—opposite "die" on the verso, I spotted "dictionary." My mother, the poststructuralist. Yes—she was, after all, French by birth. But, where to place these clovers in my unused 4th edition?

Last night she labeled this a *coterie activity*, and he saw, or thought he saw, how the omission of prairie dogs had cleared a space for resisting naturalized conceptions of arts community.

Last night we thought we were leftists, but this morning, after snuggling under the sheets together for a half hour, there was no escaping the knowledge that the only class struggle that would ever hit home would be our own.

Last night I dreamed my wife dreamt she couldn't fall asleep. To put it another way, last night my wife was a British woman who had issues with insomnia.

Last night satire didn't close on Saturday night.

Last night I wanted to be likable, but they just wouldn't let me, never mind that the counselor hated this construction.

Last night, after the worldwide collapse of world-systems theory, leading intellectuals the world over issued a moratorium on sweeping generalizations, admonishing the younger generation of intellectuals not to let economic determinism do to the twenty-first century what other forms of determinism had done to prior centuries. But, they added sagely, there was something to it.

Last night the Maginot Line collapsed, the Phoney War began, and Uncle Eric was captured by the Germans, able only at the end of the war to complete two watercolors detailing his capture, which now hang in our living room. Eric was a Frenchman through and through, but resettled with my mother's sister Ilse in Toronto, where Ilse became a Canadian citizen even as my mother resettled in the US to naturalize as a US citizen. Last night this question of betrayal by one's own country, and the subsequent ambivalence that must thereby attend to one's stubbornly patriotic longings, hung in the air as thick as melted Reblochon.

Last night I used to be a big shot. Last night you're only as good as your last story. Last night say uncle.

Last night, and then there's crowdsourcing.

Last night I had stage fright. Last night I had frostbite. Last night a state of paradoxical undress. Redress? Undress. Last night I cracked under pressure. Last night I had an upset stomach. Last night I failed a test. Last night I got divorced. Last night I went bankrupt. Last night I was dissed in public by a cherub-faced brat. Last night I tripped over my own shoelaces. Last night I watched *About Last Night*. Last night I found myself in the midst of a recursive dilemma that began "Last night," but would not end there. Last night the best laid plans. Last night an autonomic response. Last night the basal ganglia. Last night I got lost. Last night I developed carpal tunnel syndrome. Last night I stood before an audience with my fly unzipped. Last night I was arrested. Last night I was sued by—. Last night I was burglarized by—. Last night I was mugged by—. Last night I was raped by—. Last night I was assaulted by—. Last night I got fired. Last night I got drunk. Last night I got high. Last night I lost my memory. Last night I lost my mind. Last night I was despondent at the prospect of unrequited love. Last night I relinquished all hope. I chanced the streets of Constantinople last night, and last night, I died.

Se non è vero, è ben trovato.

(It needn't be true as long as it's well said.)

((Even if it's not true, it makes a good story.))

Italian proverb

Last night: that's right asshole—it's a fuckin stop sign. First you stop, then you go. You've stopped—now GO. MOVE your fuckin ass. C'mon. What the FUCK are you waiting for? You're waving ME on, Botox lady? GO. MOVE that gas-guzzling pile of shit SUV tank. You stopped before me, so first you go, then me go, just like they taught you in tank school, commando. Christallfuckinmighty, will you LOOK at this? OK, I'm going first. FUCK YOU, fuckhead. Don't even think about me waving back at you to thank you you stupid slowass FUCK. And I feel real fuckin sorry for those fuckin kids in that tank with you, they deserve a mother who can fuckin drive so at least they'll know the rules of the road when they grow up to be fuckin tank commandos like you.

Last night: oh, great—you wanna shift lanes? Why don't you run right out and pick up one of those cars that drives itself, asshole. Yeah, that way you can shift lanes without bothering to check whether someone else is there, just like you're doing now. That way you can scratch your lazy fat ass while your car shifts lanes, just like you're doing now, you witless FUCK. That's right—nice. You just cut me off to perfection, fucker, without as much as imagining there could be a car in the other lane. Without even pretending to hear my horn. And if I didn't hit my breaks, my bumper would be sitting in your lap right now. Your fat ass lap. Which means I've just saved your fat ass, your worthless fuckall fat ass, and you don't even have a clue. Hi. Yes, it's me—the guy you just cut the fuck off without knowing it? Yes, our cars are now three fuckin inches apart—I just thought I'd slow down to say hello before I continued passing your fat BMW ass at 90 mph. You can see me, right? You can see this? Uh-huh. Yes, that's right. Try not to look so astonished. You can stick this right up your fuckin fat ass. Next time you decide to drive, do us all a favor and take along your seeing-eye dog, OK? You lazy fat ass asshole.

Last night: yeah, this is nice—35 in a 55. Like my old man always said, it's always an old man with a hat. Am I supposed to feel sorry for this guy just because he's lost all hand-eye coordination? What the FUCK is he doing behind the wheel? Someone please put a bullet through my brain if I ever, EVER drive like this. What are you looking at, old man? Yeah, of course I'm passing you. Do you expect me to tailgate your ass all the way to work? What the fuck are these old men doing driving around at this hour anyway? It's like, they don't know what to do with themselves, they still get up early like they used to, so naturally they decide to drive out in the middle of morning fuckin rush hour traffic to get a fuckin cup of coffee, a fuckin donut and the fuckin newspaper that they can't even fuckin see, let alone read, fuckin up traffic wherever they go. Do us all a favor and STAY HOME, geezers. STAY THE FUCK HOME.

Last night: Jesus Christ it's fuckin bad out here. What the—don't tell me that fuckin—you'd better not—YOU FUCKIN COCK-SUCKER. YOU ROTTEN FUCKIN COCKSUCKING MOTH-ERFUCKER. Fuckin pull your piggyback rig out two feet from my front end when I can't see fuckin ten feet in front of me, just so you can say hi to your trucker pals? Fuckin truckers-are-the-best-drivers my fuckin ass. THEY SUCK and YOU SUCK WORSE, fuckwad. How is your driving? You gotta be fuckin kidding me, Mack. HOW IS YOUR FUCKIN DRIVING? You never COULD drive, fucker. Might as well ask how the fuckin US fuckin Interstate Highway System got to be a training ground for diesel-mongering blowhards, tunnel-vision millionaires with RV fever, and Sturgis rejects hoping to get laid. Now what the FUCK am I supposed to do? Wait fifteen fuckin minutes behind this fuckin son of a BITCH in fuckin whiteout conditions while he waves to each of his fuckbuddies? Fuckin stick your fuckin handles and your fuckin convoys and your fuckin tattoos and all the rest of your fuckin trucker bullshit right up your semi prick twat asses.

*

Last night: the 1960 DeSoto idles funny—the idle goes up and down inexplicably. They're sitting at the stop light on LeMoyne Ave just before the Thruway overpass. At the light beside them is what looks to be a modified '69 Dodge Dart Swinger. The older son notices that the guy's got fat tires on the rear—real fat. But that's about all he notices. They barely glance at the guy as they wait at the light together. But it's a long light, long enough to give the DeSoto time to show off its irregular idle.

Last night: the second time the DeSoto idle speeds up, the guy looks over at them, line-locks his front breaks, and steps on the gas. He smokes his back tires, the Dart letting out a terrific roar as the car body weaves left and right—but stationary, held in place by the front breaks. Then he eases off the gas.

Last night: all three of them look over at the guy—a young guy, maybe twenty-five. The father stares at the young guy, smiles, and then looks back at his sons, smiling. The DeSoto idle, having momentarily slowed, surges up again, and this time the guy in the Dart *really* steps on it, smoke pouring from his rear wheel wells, the car nosing an inch or two forward into the intersection, brakes still locked.

Last night: the three in the DeSoto start laughing, even as the young guy puts pedal closer and closer to the metal. The DeSoto idle makes a final surge, the light turns green, and the Dart leaves the intersection much as if a hurricane-force wind had scooped it up and blown it over the overpass.

Last night: as the Dart sails off, the DeSoto proceeds through the intersection at a modest rate and up the modest incline, all three of its occupants laughing, shaking their heads, knowing they won't catch as much as a glimpse of the Dart once they reach the top of the overpass.

Last night: what was that guy in the Dart thinking?

*

Last night: this Dale Earnhardt-wannabe behind me is beginning to get on my nerves. High school tassel hanging from his rearview, bobblehead sitting on his dashboard—what a fuckin douchebag. What is that piece of shit he's driving?—a restored Pinto? Maybe I should be riding *his* ass, huh? Maybe I should be riding *his* fuckin ass. That's right, Dale asshole—ride my ass just a little bit closer so I can get a good look at your acned bucktoothed face slamming into the windshield when I jam my breaks.

Last night: great—sitting here at the light alongside homes and his crew, their subwoofer is causing the fuckin change in my ashtray to rattle. This kinda shit fuckin pisses me the fuck off. First question: am I supposed to treat this as some kinda cultural difference or something? Second question: were we born with different fuckin ears? Guy driving is sitting so low in his seat that he can't even see over the dashboard, and I can't even SEE his fuckin ears, let alone his buddies' fuckin ears. What up, esé? Turn off the tunes, stop acting like someone is gonna film your fucked up life, and READ A FUCKIN BOOK, for Christsakes.

Last night: the light is GREEN, fool. Green means GO, red means STOP, just like they taught you in kindergarten. LET'S GO. Put the iPhone away, you fuckin son of a BITCH, take your other hand off your thumbdick and DRIVE THE FUCKIN CAR.

*

Last night: when he's in a hurry, which is half the time, which is NOW, he drives an automatic with two feet—one on the gas, one on the brakes. He doesn't ride the brakes, exactly—he horsewhips them. At times like these, the car surges forward from stop lights and stop signs, and he rides the bumper of the car ahead of him if it drops an iota below the speed limit—as it's doing NOW—flooring it to pass the car the instant he sees an opening, double-yellow or no—
C'mon asshole, Jesus Christ, learn how to FUCKIN drive.

Last night: they're now past the car, cruising along at 50 in a 35. They're heading south on South Bay Road. It's 9 p.m., and the roads are wet—*C'mon asshole, Jesus Christ, learn how to FUCKIN drive.*

Last night: they're heading north on Seventh North, doing 60 in a 35. It's rush hour, the roads are glazed with ice—*C'mon asshole, Jesus Christ, learn how to FUCKIN drive.*

Last night: they're heading west on Park Ave, doing 50 in a 30. It's noon on a bright summer day. The streets are dry—*C'mon asshole, Jesus Christ, learn how to FUCKIN drive.*

Last night: they're heading toward 81 on Hiawatha Boulevard, doing 80 in a 45. It's close to midnight—

*

Last night: Samuel Taylor is aware that he's written about this before, but he failed then to develop a necessary metaphor: the car Vick Sr. drives is the world he inhabits. In such a world, things, including people, are to be pushed. Hard. If they're pushed, hard, they might break, and if they break, they will thereby have satisfied expectations, thus reaffirming the status quo, that sip from the bottle held between one's legs. If they don't break, the driver will have succeeded in beating the odds, earning yet another sip from that bottle held between his legs. Passengers in the car bear witness to this struggle of a madman behind the wheel to reach his destination, his destiny, intact. They learn from his successes, his failures.

*

Last night: Vick Jr. is in a hurry, some guy in front of him is slowing him down, and Nora is sick of hearing what's running through his head—

*

Last night: must we always stand on ceremony? Answer:

*

Last night: it can't be argued with absolute authority, but it's generally agreed upon by those who study such things as scrub radii and mechanical and pneumatic trail that rear-wheel drive cars give you a better feel for the road. And a better feel for the road translates into better handling. With the exception of some newer rear-wheel drive models, however, you'd be better off with front-wheel (or four-wheel, or all-wheel) drive in a winter climate. It stands to reason that if more weight is put over the drive wheels, you'll get better traction in the snow. At least, if the vehicle is stationary. A moving vehicle complicates things, though many feel that front-wheel drive still has an edge in stop-and-go driving during wintry conditions.

Last night: but those newer rear-wheel drive vehicles?—they're a sign that rear-wheel drive is making a comeback. The newer models handle even better than their older counterparts, and they're not too bad on snow and ice, either. And of course, they have all of the advantages of newer cars—better brakes, for instance.

Last night: if you learned how to drive in a rear-wheel drive car, one of the things you presumably learned is how to handle your vehicle. In which event, you'll develop a feel for your ass end fishtailing a bit when you really hang a turn. (If you've never really hung a turn, then you haven't really learned how to handle your vehicle.) In particular, you learn to correct for fishtailing by turning your steering wheel in the direction of the skid.

Last night: if your ass end skids to the left, for instance, when you make a hard right turn, then you turn your steering wheel to the left—as much as it takes, but not more. It's a matter of judgment, of experience, and every rear-wheel drive car model behaves a bit differently, even if the basic rule—turn in the direction of the skid— remains the same.

Last night: if you learned how to drive in a rear-wheel drive car in a winter climate, you've likely found yourself doing a lot of fishtailing, a lot of correcting.

Last night: you can under-correct, and you can over-correct. Front-wheel drive is prone to understeering, or "plowing," through a turn, and rear-wheel drive is prone to oversteering, which can throw such vehicles into a spin, so drivers have to develop a feel for their vehicles.

Last night: or so does Samuel Taylor conclude, based on his field-work.

*

Last night: 1968 Chevelle. Rear-wheel drive. Two-speed "Power-glide" automatic, six-cylinder engine, two-door, turquoise body, white-top convertible. A bit worse for wear.

Last night: worse for wear or brand spanking new, everyone who owns one of these vehicles knows that if you should fishtail a bit *too* far, you're in for one *hairyass* time of it, as men of Samuel Taylor's station and generation might say. Has to do with the overall design of the car, its weight distribution, suspension system, steering assembly. Your ass end slides out beyond a certain point, and recovering the sucker—as men of Samuel Taylor's station and generation who grew up in Central New York might call it—is nigh impossible.

Last night: Vick Jr. knew all this heading north on Rt. 81—Interstate 81 in today's lingo—that morning on his way to work. He knew all this, but was at the time preoccupied with other things—chiefly, his growing dissatisfaction with the way his life was turning out—and wasn't paying especially close attention to the road conditions on this chilly, sunny, December morning. He reaches down absentmindedly to change the radio station.

Last night: Rt. 81 northbound curves to the right a short distance before the Rt. 481 exit that Vick takes every morning, and just as Vick approaches this curve in the outside lane, he notices a soft glare on the road. But it isn't until midway through the turn that he real-izes what's about to happen, at which realization the ass end of his Chevelle begins to slide out to the left.

Last night: he's been here before, but not at 65 mph, and not this deep into a turn.

Last night: *Life's been*

Last night: instantly alive to his predicament, Vick flicks his wheel quickly to the left by a palm's width, stopping the skid for a moment, but just for a moment. As he comes around the turn, the Chevelle ass end swings hard now to the right.

Last night: *good to*

Last night: Vick can see traffic ahead of him, and behind him, but about all he can do at this point is try again to stop the slide by turning the wheel a palm's width to the right.

Last night: *me so*

Last night: the Chevelle body comes sliding again to the left, but this time with such force that no amount of correction by Vick can stop it from spinning all the way around.

Last night: *far*

Last night: Vick is now facing the oncoming traffic, sliding ass end first down 81 at more than 60 mph. He tries to slow his vehicle by hitting, then releasing the brake pedal several times, giving him momentary traction as he maneuvers the car the best he can out of the outside lane and toward the inside lane of the highway, where his car, if he's lucky, can come to rest between the guardrail and the inside lane without obstructing traffic. This requires crossing three lanes of sporadic traffic while moving backwards, facing the traffic.

Last night: there's a short period of time—perhaps several seconds—during this backward-forward motion that, his efforts to maneuver his vehicle largely lost now to the ice, Vick can do little but sit and watch as oncoming traffic maneuvers around *him*, the vehicle inching closer and closer to the guardrail as a result of its momentum. Somewhere in the back of his mind he hears but doesn't quite identify a familiar commercial jingle now playing on the radio. It's during this period that Vick feels both aware of his situation and curiously distant from it. He's being carried into the future on glare ice, the absence of friction, of resistance to backward-forward motion, amounting to a lack of control over his own immediate circumstances and final, if not terminal, destination. It's a situational cliché not lost on Vick at the moment of his participation in it, life flashing before his eyes not as life exactly, but as narrated life, that odd variant of the examined life examined under the auspices of story. Vick realizes that, at this moment, both his daily routine and his life story are in the midst of being replotted, to what degree and in what fashion it being anyone's guess.

Last night: he smiles to himself.

Last night: and just as Vick smiles to himself, his vehicle finally reaches the guardrail, the front left fender of his Chevelle striking into the steel barrier with such impact that the vehicle is knocked 180 degrees around, sliding to a stop between the guardrail and the inside lane—aside from the impact, just as Vick had imagined—and once again facing in the direction of traffic.

Last night: Vick gets out of his vehicle, careful not to open his door into the oncoming traffic that has slowed to rubberneck and, in some cases, to switch from the inside to the center lane, in the process slipping and sliding past Vick's vehicle at all angles. One eye on the traffic and one on his own vehicle, Vick examines his crushed left fender—he sees immediately that the $300 Chevelle is totaled—and just as he considers what his next move might be, a Dodge wagon comes careening around the iced curve, the driver panicking at the site of the Chevelle, hitting her breaks too hard, and forcing her car into a slide that puts it square into the guardrail just behind Vick's car. The driver pops out of her vehicle, running this way and that to examine the damage. She's an Asian woman who evidently speaks little English, and in her frenzy she ends up situating herself behind her car, with her back to the oncoming traffic, holding her face and moaning while dipping slightly up and down at the waist. She's not physically hurt, Vick concludes, but if she doesn't get out from behind that wagon, she's got a good chance of being clipped by oncoming traffic. He gently takes the woman's arm in his and coaxes her to follow him around to the front of his vehicle.

Last night: just then a state trooper appears at the scene. Another car slides sideways around the curve even as the trooper gets out of his car—the driver manages to recover from the skid—and the trooper radios the road crews to get some salt and sand on the curve. *Now.*

*

Last night: does Vick Jr. have what it takes to be a writer?

*

Last night: on which album did "Highway Star" first appear?

*

Last night: is it OK if you're just along for the ride?

*

Last night: yes. Or so does Samuel Taylor conclude, based on his fieldwork.

*

Last night: 1986 Escort. Automatic, front-wheel drive, two-door, silver and grey. Good in the snow.

Last night: eastbound on I-90, not far from Erie PA. Really more like northeast-bound. Night. Been drivin for eight hours now. Clear till now, but now it's snowin like there's no tomorrow. Tryin to keep it at 75 mph anyway, but the shit is comin down so hard that it's gettin difficult to see.

Last night:
Gonna free fall out into nothin.
Keep your eyes on the road.
Gonna leave this world for a while.
Eyes on the road.
Eyes
on

the

road, motherfucker. On the road. Stay alert, try not to think too hard about it.

Free fallin.

Free. Fallin? Fallin. Fallen. Free? Yes and no.

What are you sayin? Talkin to yourself.

Doesn't wanna let up. Hope this is just local lake effect. Fuckin Erie—same fuckin story every fuckin time you pass this fuckin place. Take it easy.

Those Christmas lights in the middle of that field? Must be lonely out on the farm this time of year, huh Zeke? Moo.

Must be goin nuts.

Drive. On the road. Eyes.

"I'm your vehicle baby." Yeah, but you can't sing worth a shit.

Goddamn wind is pickin up, more northwest than west. Just fuckin great.

Hope Mike is OK. Wish you coulda been there. Shoulda been there yourself.

Maybe you'll give Nancy a call when you get into town. Tomorrow maybe.

No—shouldn't. She's a nice girl, deserves more—

Attention? Fuck it. Could use some easy pussy, and hers fits your dick like a glove. Starts comin the second you're inside her. And her asshole is what you call *hungry*—takes it nice from behind. Tasty little fuckhole too, even with your come oozin out of it. Hear she's Tony Numbnuts' fuckshop now, but hey—she'll always be your pig.

Jesus, gettin hard just thinkin about it. Might have her suck you off *after* you stick her in the ass. Wonder if she's got any—

JESUS–

FUCKNUTS!

SHIT! That was close. Gotta watch the road. Fuck that Nancy shit. Bad out here, gotta make it home tonight.

Callin her tomorrow, first thing.

What was that? Did that jock say from Buffalo east to Syracuse? Shit.

There goes another plow. At least they don't mess around up this

way, unlike those pussies back in Illinois.
On all fours, oh yeah, right up the ass.

Last night:
Buffalo just around the bend here. The wind should be behind
you after that.
Man, weather's gettin even worse. Fuckin some heavy shit comin
down.
Kinda pretty though, everything covered in white. Miss this part
of the world.
Yeah, for about two seconds. If you had to put up with this shit
every other day—
Wouldn't be bad though if you could vacate from, say, January
through March.
Fuck that.
Huh, city looks quiet. No cars.
This is one Popeyed town.
OK, wind's behind me now. On the home stretch. Only another
two-and-a-half hours if you can keep it above 60.
Road is for shit though. Plows just aren't keeping up with it, and
they're using those big suckers with the spreaders. Good thing this
little shitbox is front-wheel drive.

Last night:
What is that?—early Traffic, with Mason? Haven't heard that
one in a while, good tune.
CHRIST!
SHIT! Nearly lost it there. Concentrate. Eyes
on
the
road.
On the road. Jesus Christ this is bad in through here, better slow
it down some. Wind is sweeping across out of the north now—fuckin
lake effect bullshit.
45 and you're still all over the place. Like glass underneath this
shit. Musta had some freezing rain or sleet or some shit.

Gotta slow it down even more here. Shit. Almost a little sleepy. Fuck that.

Just get home, get to bed, deal with it all tomorrow. Try to get some sleep. Ilse and Serge coming in tomorrow, and Dominick.

The hell with alla that—sleep first.

Wonder what it'll be like to see everybody?

Will you look at this fuckin asshole. 30 in the passing lane.

That's right asshole, I'm goin around you now, try not to get nervous and end up in the median.

Bye-bye.

Fuckin Coupe de Ville imbeciles have no business out on the road if they can't handle their vehicles.

Cornhole her right up the ass, yeah. Says she loves that Vick dick.

Maybe you should pull over at this rest stop and phone Mike, tell him you'll be getting in late.

Good idea.

Man, this place is deserted. Look at this shit comin down.

Last night:

Mike?—yeah, hey. Yeah, it's fuckin bad. Got maybe another hundred miles, but at this rate, it'll be another three hours. How's it there?

Eight inches? Shit. Figures. Well, car is doin OK anyway.

Right, yeah, I'm not in a rush, believe me.

Godard? That crazy fucker is back in town? We should all get shitfaced.

Yeah.

OK. So I'll take it slow and get there when I get there. You want me to call you when I get in? Might be pretty late.

OK. Yeah, alright, I'll give you a call when I'm in.

See ya soon. Bye.

Last night:

Gonna have to bring back a lot of stuff when you leave. Have to pack this shitbox to the brim. Hope the rolltop will fit. Mike'll give you a hand with it.

Stop worrying about that stuff. First things first.

Fuckin Godard. Crazy fucker. Mike's gonna wanna climb the Gunks with him, and he's gonna want you to go along.

Fuck that climbing shit. Get a broken ankle just thinking about it.

Wind is back in your face. Jesus Christ how is that even *possible*? Don't look at the snowflakes—look at the road.

On the road.

Wonder how the apartment's gonna look. Didn't look all that great three weeks ago. Probably have to clean it up first, while you're busy emptying it. After tomorrow.

Tomorrow is gonna be one longass day. Wish you could do it exactly the way he'd wanted, but with all of the family there—

But goddamn you wish you could skip the Catholic bullshit. Mike feels the same.

Hope they find a way to cover your classes for the next two weeks.

Just can't think about that now.

Not a soul out here.

Wonder who'll show up for the services. Little fuckin Italy, probably. Hope you can place the faces.

Nobody out here, not a soul. Easier this way.

Last night:

OK, let's see. Hell with 690, may as well just take this all the way to Thompson Road. Good ole exit 35. Then circle back to the apartments.

Shit, 1:00 a.m. already.

Hope they salted that hill up to James Street. That can be a bitch.

Last night:

Hi. Here you go.

Thanks, have a good one.

Last night:

Miserable fuckin job. Workin for the state maybe, but miserable.

Jesus Christ—must be a foot of snow on the ground. Where the fuck are the plows? Slippery as hell too. Streets are deserted.

Well, Carrier looks pretty much the same. Wonder how long *that'll* last.

Gut ache all of a sudden. Wish I'd had the time this morning to take that third shit.

OK, c'mon car, let's go.

C'MON.

Last night:

Man that was close. If you didn't blow that red at the top of the hill you woulda never made it.

Huh, seemed easier to get up that hill in my old Nova. More weight at that grade on the rear end?

Barely caught a glimpse of Bristol. Could smell it though.

Fuckin shithole, penicillin or no penicillin. Fuck that place.

Right up the ass, nice girl or no nice girl.

Last night:

Should be smooth sailin now.

The Palace. When was it you went with Mom to *Babbette's Feast*? Was that '89, or '88?

Had to be '89. Great flick.

OK, here's Grant. Not long now.

Last night:

Alrighty then, just around the bend.

This is it.

Shit, fucking lot isn't plowed. Figures.

Better get out and have a look.

Last night:

Don't know about this.

Fuck it, give it a try.

Last night:

C'mon car.

C'MON.
Fuck this. Gunnin it.
C'MON.

Last night:
FUCK.
OK. You're stuck, and blocking the entrance, just where the pavement rises a cunt hair or two.
Fuck. Get out and see what's what.
Uh-huh. You can put it in drive and this little front-wheel-drive shitbox sits in place with the front wheel spinnin. Too slippery, and too much snow underneath the chassis.

Last night:
OK then. So put it in neutral, open the door, get out, and rock the car by pushin against the door jam. When you get it to roll a coupla feet each way and just as it's about to roll backward, hop in, slap it into drive and gun it. You've done this with every shitbox you've ever owned, you can handle it.

Last night:
C'mon.
C'MON.
FUCK
YOU.
Fuckin slipperyass
SHIT, goddamn
it.

Last night:
Shit, nearly took your back out. Too much sittin on your ass behind the wheel to be jumpin right into this kinda shit.
Too much fuckin wear and tear.
Too much. Too fuckin much. Just too fuckin much of too much for anyone to be doin this kind of SHIT.

Last night:

Must look like a fuckin dummy, sittin on your ass in the snow.

Yeah, like anyone is awake. Fuckin geriatric ward.

Get on all fours to stand or you'll only end up on your ass again, dumbshit.

Hands raw already.

Definitely makin that phone call tomorrow, first thing. Have that little whore lick your balls.

OK, gather your wits, you stupid fuck. One more time.

C'MON.

That's it.

THAT"S

IT.

Here

we

GO.

FLOOR IT.

DRIVE.

REVERSE.

DRIVE.

REVERSE.

DRIVE.

C'MON.

Fuck it. That was close. Nearly dropped the transaxle.

But you're in OK.

So OK then, so we're here, FINALLY.

Home sweet fuckin home.

Last night:

Beat. One long fuckin day. Or night. Or whatever.

Grab your books outta the back seat, carry your shit upstairs, call Mike, and try to catch some shuteye. You're gonna need to be good and rested up for tomorrow's fuckass casket affair. Fuckin steel, no less. He said he didn't want an open casket—all he wanted, wood-worker that he was, was a pine fuckin box—but with his brothers

there and all—
    Man, lucky you got front-wheel drive.

3   LAST NIGHT

Nothing is so perfectly amusing as a total change of ideas.

Laurence Sterne

Last night, to flesh out the circumstances of Samuel Taylor's life at this moment in time requires a few stage props—domestic arrangement, income and assets. These consist of the following: a spouse, tenure-track; a job, non-tenure-track; a $110,000 townhouse, bank-owned; furniture, owned; a used car, owned; a used Mac and a new Mac, the former owned, the latter property of the university; 1347 books, owned; savings in the amount of $25,285 and change; credit card debt in the amount of $21,564; total retirement savings of nearly $100,000. $5000 in equity.

*

Last night, Samuel Taylor gets down on his hands and knees to weed his yard. This is not something the author would do, but it might be something his narrator would do. Samuel Taylor's wife wants them to go green, and he respects the green imperative himself. So he's weeding their yard by hand. The tiny front lawn abuts the front lawn of the townhouse directly to the east, and his easterly neighbor uses weed killer and fertilizer to produce an impeccable patch of green. Samuel Taylor's lawn has never been properly maintained—it's overgrown with weeds, "more weeds than grass," he likes to say. Before he and his wife bought the townhouse, they rented it from absentee landlords, and his neighbor had been good enough to mow their lawn. So Samuel Taylor now feels obliged to create a seamless patch of green comprised of his and his neighbor's tiny front lawns. As for the backyard, he will do the same, but the landlord who owns the two units adjacent to theirs to the west—theirs is a four-unit, "zero lot line" structure, the westernmost unit occupied by a family whose breadwinner owns his unit, and helped to build the structure—is not mowing or maintaining that portion of the backyard, and so Samuel Taylor remembers the Frost poem, and builds accordingly. Or, has others build for him, for a fee. A thousand miles further west and a time zone earlier, the Foothills rise out of nowhere, commencing a permeable membrane that separates the vast expanse of Midwestern plain and prairie from another kind of terrain, another history of land disputes. Samuel Taylor and his wife have arrived here from that other history, at which other history they had arrived from still other histories.

*

Last night, a month goes by. Samuel Taylor is still weeding his yard by hand, planting a mix of grass seed and soil and green-sanctioned fertilizer where he digs out each weed or clump of weeds, and watering every day. He's now purchased a number of tools to supplement his efforts: electric plug-in lawn mower (identical to his neighbor's), weed wacker, hedge trimmers, clippers, shovel, rake, spreader, hose, hose rack, lawn sprinkler, spade, work gloves. He buys most of these items at one of those large home and building supply chains. He tries not to spend an inordinate amount of time investigating best buys and consumer reports—he doesn't want to get caught up in that buying frenzy that seems to be the hallmark of the upper quintiles— but finds himself stumped at times as to making the right purchase. After hunting the aisles for the lawn sprinkler section, he's greeted by a sizable array of plastic devices, ranging in price from four dollars to twenty-five dollars. He picks up the yellow four-buck item. He likes the color—reminds him of the yellow swirling sprinkler he and his brother would jump through as kids while their mother picked through her rose petals for beetles, dropping them into a coffee can containing a splash of gasoline. His mother used to plant tomatoes and chives along the side of their house, and he'd take a saltshaker outside with him occasionally, pull a tomato from the vine, and eat it standing there. Dolores Terrace South, or South Dolores Terrace? Nice sprinkler, especially for the price. He flips it over. "Made in China." He's got nothing against China. His eye scans down the next few sprinklers, and he recognizes a green item, larger than the four-buck sprinkler, a little sturdier. He's seen a lot of these in his neighborhood, which he takes as a sign that they're dependable. Only thing is, it's twenty bucks. He flips it over. "Made in USA," next to which, a small sticker of an American flag. He feels suddenly that it's incumbent upon him to make a moral choice. A choice upon which will turn the wealth of nations. A choice he'll be reminded of each time he waters his lawn. He carries one of the sprinklers to the self-check-out register. Is this what you call fidelity? he wonders. Or is it chauvinism? Or is it charity?

*

Last night, Samuel Taylor sits on the shady part of their second-story deck, the sun having just fallen behind their house, "Dancing Days" playing on the small boom box in their living room. The volume is too low for this kind of music, he thinks. He can just make out the chchch chuh chchc chuh chchchc chuh of a keyboard struck at a wonted tempo, the murmur of their refrigerator. She's working on her novel again, he thinks. He peers out across the adjoining backyards, which slope gently down to touch at the easement, a suburban canyon of chain link, yelping dog, smoking barbecue grills, and patterned concealment extending to the cottonwoods that block the eastern horizon. Nobody owns those cottonwoods, he thinks, or we all do. Like everyplace but one place, this place reminds him of someplace else.

*

Last night, Samuel Taylor begins his new novel. "In the pages that follow," he writes, "everyone lives. Meaning, everyone dies." This is as far as he's gotten. He weighs the pros and cons of assigning an epigraph to each chapter of the novel. Googling "epigraph," he stumbles upon a blog exchange in which the consensus would seem to be contra. But demarcation appeals to him more and more these days, so he begins to collect epigraphs for chapters that do not yet exist. He gazes out the window of his home office, south past the stretch of chain link that divides his new suburban tract from the older, low-income apartments immediately across the street. Demarcation appeals to him more and more these days, and some of his friends mistake his impatience with social dishabille—in particular, with the trash that blows across the street from the apartments, littering his bushes and yard—as a growing misanthropy stemming from his recent professional travail. The chief obstacle to integration, he speculates, is a failure to confront directly the benefits of boundaries. And boundaries ought to be a matter more of respect for one's cohabitants than a physical or legal barrier, he thinks. Ought to be, he thinks. But who wants to live around poverty? Certainly not those who were once poor, he assures himself. The sky is hazy. Thirty miles south sits a nuclear reactor, its 5000-acre cooling reservoir boasting one of the few beaches in this part of the state. Standing along the shore of the lake in the hot July twilight shortly after their move here, Samuel Taylor and his wife struggle to put a good face on oblivion.

*

Last night, one must confess, it's not his ideas one doesn't like—it's his attitude. He's a snob and, even worse, a whiner. He's no westerner. He should go back to where he came from originally, east, or north, or northeast, where he can take out that urban aggression of his on the elite art he claims to like, and where he can cook his macaroni dishes for Guidos who think it's a main course. Lincoln said that at forty you have the face you deserve. Will you get a load of those scowl lines? What is he so bitter about? Everyone experiences setbacks, and his life has gone better than most. Talk about ungrateful. Little wonder he's ended up where he has.

*

Last night, at the center of the Land of Lincoln, one does not always know what one is thinking. This first week of yard work has proved tougher than he'd imagined, blisters erupting on each hand between his thumb and forefinger. For some minutes now, a large robin has been watching him from behind a bush. There are no hills, making it difficult to gain perspective, even if natives allege that the big sky, agribiz aside, makes it easier for them to breathe. He'd read somewhere about the monk parrots that nest year-round in Hyde Park, Chicago, sometimes building large nests around electrical transformers. Such nests have been known to cause power outages, so ComEd is sometimes forced to tear one down, usually to public protest. Parrots in other urban areas—Brooklyn, San Francisco—have created similar problems. But birds will be birds, and non-native species find ways to adapt. That robin is still there. What does he want? What's keeping him here? Can one know what one knows?

*

Last night, another month goes by. Samuel Taylor is still weeding his yard by hand, planting a mix of grass seed and soil and green-sanctioned fertilizer where he digs out each weed or clump of weeds, and watering every day. The lawn is coming along pretty well, but the region has fallen into drought conditions, so watering the new seedlings is a must. Each and every morning, first thing, Samuel Taylor dons his yard work outfit—a pair of shorts, an old tee, a baseball cap he picked up on their trip to the Black Hills, and a beat-up pair of running sneaks—and sets about the task of hooking up his hose to his Made-in-USA sprinkler, watering first the front lawn, then the narrow side yard, then the backyard, at least twenty minutes each. He picks up litter and leaves as he goes about his business, and yanks out strands of small hop clover. He remembers small hop clover from Dolores Terrace South, or South Dolores Terrace. After watering, he and his wife have breakfast together. Then chchch chuh chchc chuh chchchc chuh.

*

Last night, they sit together sipping coffee on the shady part of their second-story deck, summer months of morning sun having bleached the other half of the deck, NPR's Morning Edition playing on the small boom box in their living room. What are you working on next? she says. I'm not sure, he says. I've got an idea for a new book. Why don't you work on that? she says. I need a better way in, he says. And I just haven't found it. That old piece of yours, "Last night," is really great, she says. Doesn't fit with what I have in mind, he says. And anyway. What's wrong? she says. I'm enjoying the yard stuff, he says. I think I need the break. I think you're depressed, she says. I'm not depressed, he says. I'm just sick of the situation I'm in. I'm sick of these discussions, she says. I know, he says. But I can't help the way I feel. I don't think these drugs I'm taking are working, she says. You mean for the bronchitis, he says? Drink more water. Not the bronchitis, dummy, she says. You remember that postcard you sent me when you were hiking in the Alps, the one with the poem on it? he says. Just like Brahms and Clara Schumann, only the reverse. It wasn't a postcard, it was an email, and I was in the Rockies, she says. Oh, he says. Is it evening yet? I think so, she says. But it's getting late, that much is certain.

*

Last night, Samuel Taylor begins his new novel. "In the pages that follow," he writes, "everyone dies. Meaning, life goes on." This is as far as he's gotten. Of late he's noticed what appears to be the same large robin hiding every morning behind his backyard bushes. Natives say that cardinals and blue jays are among the most stunning birds in these parts. But since the Mississippi forms the western border of the state, they live not all that far from the migratory flyway. On a trip to Chicago the summer prior, they'd spotted a lone bald eagle hovering above I-55 near the Kankakee River. They are the kind of people who take such a sighting at face value, but can't help wishing it a good omen. Like that large white owl perched atop the telephone pole as they exited the Hotel Boulderado that evening after her Naropa debut. They are the kind of people who would rather read the book of nature than believe in God, but can't really bring themselves to do either.

*

Last night, one must confess, he needs to open up. To someone. On a regular basis. Else his anger will not abate. Else he'll kill her.

*

Last night, at the center of the Land of Lincoln, one does not always know what one is thinking. His back and hips are stiff and achy. For days now, a large robin has been pecking away at his grass seed. He's taken to squirting the creature with his garden hose, but it hops behind the bushes to avoid the spray. If he chases the bird, it flies to the periphery of his yard or alights atop a neighbor's roof, returning the moment he goes inside. What keeps him here? There can't be too much seed left. Growing old together, sharing sweet sorrow, spying on each other, makes sense to him most days. The future makes sense to him most days. He would like those closest to him to know that he is content in his own thoughts, his own body. He would like those closest to him to know that his desperation is merely his awareness that what lies in wait is, finally, unanswerable. For us all. More music, he urges. For us all. More laughter. Beyond that, we have the robin to consider. The robin, kept here by something, he is sure of it. But what? Beneath—

*

Last night, another month goes by. Samuel Taylor is still weeding his yard by hand, planting a mix of grass seed and soil and green-sanctioned fertilizer where he digs out each weed or clump of weeds, and watering every day. The drought has continued, as has chchch chuh chchc chuh chchchc chuh. The lawn is at last looking like a lawn, and his next-door neighbors are looking at him like he's a little *too* industrious. His forearms, legs and neck are deeply tanned, and the work has shaken off five pounds. Another semester is about to start. The future.

*

Last night, Nora sits alone on their second-story deck, in the shade, coughing now and then and sipping water, the afternoon sun falling behind their house, "Rocky Mountain High" playing on the small boom box in their living room. The volume is too low for this kind of music, she thinks. She can just make out the chuh chchch chuh chchch chuh of a keyboard struck at a wonted tempo, the murmur of their refrigerator. He's doing email again, she thinks. She spots a robin, peering at her from below. Probably that bird that keeps pestering him, she thinks. Having just finished a draft of her novel, she wonders when he'll start writing something substantial again. What else are summers for? she thinks. Nora's favorite dish is Penne alla Kassia, which Samuel Taylor taught her how to make. Typically Nora bakes the bread, but tonight she'll be cooking the meal too. A light salad after would be nice, she thinks. He'd like that. She's reminded of how often he talks about the health benefits of salads, and how they make even an ordinary meal special. Just then she remembers that she has yet to fill out her application for additional life insurance, but she quickly goes back to thinking about supper. She peers out across the adjoining backyards, which slope gently down to touch at the easement, a suburban canyon of newlyweds, crying kids, squeaking swing sets and potted flowers extending to the cottonwoods that block the eastern horizon. Most of these couples probably work for State Farm, she thinks. Like everyplace but one place, this place reminds her of someplace else.

*

Last night, Samuel Taylor begins his new novel. "In the pages that follow," he writes, "everyone is in love. Meaning, smoke gets in your eyes." This is as far as he's gotten. He's just given an email interview to an online journal in which he's claimed that, although he's certainly been influenced by his peers, his primary inspiration is not the work of other authors. With regard to other writing he's something of a parasite, he's explained, picking up techniques or stratagems he can use in his own compositions, but also, to borrow from Michel Serres's influential treatise, making a pest of himself through allusion, insinuating his doubts into discourses operating at a remove from his own. His true sources of inspiration have more to do with pop culture—music and film in particular—and the lives he's led. How many lives *have* you led? the interviewer had asked. Samuel Taylor had answered "three." His wife likes the number three. *Leaves of three, let it be*, his lips silently wrap around the words. He pores over his growing catalog of epigraphs. *If a man will begin with certainties, he shall end in doubts; but if he will be content to begin with doubts he shall end in certainties. I hear and I forget; I see and I remember; I write and I understand. When in Rome, do as you done in Milledgeville. Immigration is the sincerest form of flattery. What is a cynic? A man who knows the price of everything, and the value of nothing. Any authentic work of art must start an argument between the artist and his audience. Stay uncommercial. There's a lot of money in it. Great art works, being unique, are final: they do not open doors, they close them. But with the works of art of our own present age, university study tends to accelerate the process by which the radical and subversive work becomes the classic work. Be cheerful while you are alive.* Be cheerful while you are alive. He thinks of the robin, the robin redbreast of his youth.

*

Last night, one must confess, revision ought to demand other than to flinch in the face of the truth.

*

Last night, at the center of the Land of Lincoln, one does not always know what one is thinking. He'd been logy of late, the lawn having sapped more of his energies than he'd anticipated. Chchch chuh chchc chuh chchchc chuh. He was trying to concentrate on an article about Fermat when he thought he remembered a word, "fermata," but couldn't recall what it meant. Every time he looked up a word, he stumbled upon a new word. Last time it was "dendrochronology." He liked looking up words, telling his friends that it was a sign of humility. Just as he stood to get his new dictionary, a bird darted out from under the deck, landing in the bushes. It was the robin. He walked down the deck stairs to the backyard, and ducked under the deck to see what was what. It wasn't quite tall enough for him to stand, and he had to watch he didn't bump his head on the two-by-sixes. Nothing caught his eye. He turned to walk back up, and then he spotted it—a small nest of twigs and bits of grass sitting atop the electric meter box, flush up against the aluminum siding. He walked up and tried to get his head between the nest and the underside of the deck to peer inside, the robin following his every move, but there wasn't enough room. He walked back upstairs to retrieve a small handheld mirror. Careful not to disturb the nest, he held the mirror against the siding and angled it to see inside. In the mirror's reflection he saw, tucked in the nest, three tiny turquoise eggs. In the mirror's reflection he saw beginnings, middles, and ends. In the mirror's reflection he saw what he wanted to see.

4   TONIGHT

Whatever it is we enjoy about stories, we enjoy them because we forget they *are* stories. We have given ourselves over to something greater than mere form. And, no matter how cleverly you try, if you point that out to us, you break that fragile spell. End of story.

> Joseph Salvatore reviewing Douglas Coupland's *Generation A* in *The New York Times Book Review*, January 10, 2010

Tonight, February hogs were up, and Samuel Taylor decided it was high time to hang up his jock strap.

Tonight, a lame duck occupied the Oval Office. But Samuel Taylor's decision to quit the trade—or, the trade as defined by how he had grown accustomed to plying it—had little if anything to do with hogs or ducks. Ditto bulls, bears, elephants, donkeys, snakes-in-the-grass. Pigs too. It was the Year of the Pig, which could be taken somewhat too literally to mean, Year of the Immature Hog. But immature or full-grown, hogs amounted, at most, to a positive correlation.

Tonight, Samuel Taylor tended to blame everything on globalization. Out of work? Globalization. Corruption? Globalization. Poor gas mileage? Globalization. No privacy? Globalization. Spam? Globalization. Dog-eat-more-dog? Globalization. Too many guns? Globalization. Too many drugs? Globalization. Too many books? Globalization. Too many bombs? Globalization. Bad manners? Globalization. No sex drive? Globalization. Lack of fiber in your diet? Globalization. Complexion spotty? Globalization. Johnny can't read? Globalization. Johnny can't breathe? Globalization. Death and taxes? Globalization. Global warming? Globalization. Creationism? Globalization. Corporatization? Globalization. Globalization? Globalization.

Tonight, if it wasn't the animal kingdom that was knocking the wind out of Samuel Taylor's sails, stealing the piss from his vinegar, leaving him grasping for metaphors beyond his reach, neither was it globalization.

Tonight, Samuel Taylor's problem was him, or to be more precise, his *memory*. His memory: it couldn't be avoided, anymore than he could avoid writing, so many years later, about his decision to put a provisional end to his writing career. That's the thing about memory: even when you turn your attention to present mysteries, it's not as if you've forgotten your past. Thanks to the amygdala or the hippocampus or to Mnemosyne herself, something inside, a circulatory something that coordinates those strange exchanges of neural energy animating the brain, *something* remembers, even when you're busy not. Proust certainly understood as much. And when you *do* forget, and when you forget that you've forgotten, who can deny that the work of forgotten memory continues to play a role in who you are, and are in the process of becoming?

Tonight, Samuel Taylor was in the process of becoming—to put the obligatory fine point on it—not a writer, finally, but a *storyteller*. Which is why, when February hogs were up and intensities of all sorts were multiplying, he decided it was high time to hang up his jock strap.

*

Tonight, it's cold out. Carl's Drugs is just closing up for the night, its storefront dimming as he hangs a left at the light and heads north up Electronics Parkway. He's killing time, taking the long way home.

Tonight, the radio is off. Patches of ice cover the road, but his mind is elsewhere. He's trying to think, but he's uncertain as to what he's really trying to think about—maybe the job, probably the job, he thinks. Trying to get a fix on the Big Picture, maybe. Can't be sure. Christmas is right around the corner.

Tonight, he accelerates only a few hundred feet after the turn before he just catches a glimpse of a shadow moving along the shoulder of the road—a lopsided gait, head bobbing up and down. As he passes, the shadow turns and pokes out a right hand in universal hitchhiker silhouette. He makes him out to be an old guy. Something about him.

Tonight, his mind is elsewhere, so it takes him a moment to register this passing figure—and another moment, as it usually does, to convince himself it's just a ride he's after. Besides, it's an old guy. So he swings the car over to the side of the road, and waits, foot on the brakes. He can see the old guy in his rearview, hustling up the eighty odd feet to the car, his head bobbing up and down a little *too* vigorously.

Tonight, he reaches over and pushes open the passenger side door. The door swings open just as the old guy reaches it. This close, he can make out the light frost that coats a few weeks' worth of greying beard. He can see the frays in his weathered overcoat. He looks to be a man of sixty. He's breathing heavily, each puff condensing, then disappearing into the warm car. His left arm is bent and positioned, awkwardly, behind his back, and he's stooped forward a bit, favoring the right side of his body. He leans in to speak.

*

Tonight, to concentrate simply on telling stories, to make the story and its arc one's primary aim, is in some sense to take the value of narrative for granted as a means of entertaining one's readers, or more fundamentally, of holding their attention.

Tonight, or so Samuel Taylor had concluded, based on his fieldwork.

Tonight, and during that January of years past, when hog futures were up, it had occurred to him that there was plenty of room on our fiercely globalizing planet for taking some things for granted, narrative included, and for holding attention, and for entertaining. And tonight he decided that, push come to shove, first and foremost, he wanted to entertain.

Tonight, he wanted to hold attention.

Tonight, he wanted to take some things for granted.

Tonight, he wanted to tell stories.

Tonight, globalization?

Tonight, it's not as if the divide between writers and storyteller-entertainers was then, or is now, a neat and tidy one, or that every nuance attendant to the word "writing" can be understood via such a dichotomy. There are writers who tell stories for whom the telling of stories is not the primary aim; and there are storyteller-entertainers whose tales are not without conceptual heft. Writers of both stripes might ask us to consider not only where the stories are going to, but where the stories are coming from. Where the words are going to, and where they're coming from. Both camps might ask us to consider this strange stuff we call language, every bit as strange perhaps as those exchanges of neural energy animating the brain. But by and large, storyteller-entertainers were far more invested in rendering language transparent—a transparent medium through which a reader might be transported to untold representational or ideational coordinates. Yes, this is what such tribes wanted—they wanted to take their readers somewhere, to places foreign to the text itself.

Tonight, or so Samuel Taylor had concluded, based on his fieldwork.

*

Tonight, they're at Heid's. The place is mobbed, but Vick Sr. moves through the line quickly. Meantime, Mikey and his brother arch their heads this way and that, trying to see through the trees that hover over Heid's, obscuring the Lakeshore Drive-in screen. Mikey eyes one tree carefully, a twisted maple, even at this young age thinking about what it might take to hoist himself up to the top branch. The Lakeshore is playing *Dr. No*, but Mikey and his brother won't really discover Bond until *Goldfinger*, and at an indoor second-run theater, the Hollywood. On this humid summer evening, the Heid's parking lot is packed with young people a decade older than the two boys, many sitting on the hoods of their cars and craning their necks to catch the action on *and* off the screen.

Tonight, Vick Sr. scooches back into the '52 Olds bench seat, balancing in his right hand a donut box stuffed with hot dogs, a bag each of pretzels and chips, drinks, and a wad of napkins. Suzie lowers the glove box lid, picks out her birch beer and sets it in the space provided. After a bit of finessing, Vick Sr. turns and reaches over the seat to hand his sons a frank and a Coney, each wrapped in a napkin. Then he hands his older son the bag of pretzels, and his younger son the chips, and both their drinks, which they rest on the vinyl space between them.

Tonight, the boys aren't listening to the father squawk to the mother about having been given "end rolls" by the Heid's counter staff. They're too busy tearing open their cartons of chocolate milk, washing down their mustard-coated missiles.

Tonight, they linger in the lot, the mother and the father talking about the father's job at the shop, whether the mother should go back to work at the factory to help the father with bills. A train horn sounds in the distance. In a few minutes it'll pass behind the screen. But by then they'll be on their way back home. Up Old Liverpool Road, a left on Electronics Parkway—

Tonight, it's the same road Vick is on now, 7th North, repaved and renamed to suit the General Electric Corporation, which at one time employed over ten thousand workers at their Liverpool plant alone. Vick Sr. worked there, while Suzie worked at the Court Street plant. This was before the divorce.

*

Tonight, to accuse a writer of waxing "self-conscious" was tantamount to deeming him too…self-conscious, ill at ease with his own writerly wares, indulging in a reflexive variant of irony of the sort that few readers would perceive as anything but a *gimmick*. There was craft implicit in the writing act, and the point of the writer's craft was to woo readers away from apprehending the very devices that these self-conscious tribes insisted on flaunting, many of which devices, in any case—or so went the popular argument, which gradually became axiomatic—had been done to death. Whereas storytellers—storytellers were thought by most readers, and by most writers, to be entirely comfortable with their own inclinations, as indeed most were. Comprising a bestseller majority, after all, few were especially inclined to question their privileged hold on the public's retromodernist or Victorian or just plain limited imagination. As a consequence, the word *natural* was often ascribed to these scribes, sometimes by these selfsame scribes. "Self-conscious" writers thus grew prone to arguing, in their own defense, for the benefits of *de*naturalization, not infrequently aligning their efforts with the presumably nobler enterprise of inciting more active reading, heightening social awareness, subverting the status quo, unmasking the flows of global capital, and so forth, all via the striking of authorial pose in consciously reflexive prose.

Tonight, as Samuel Taylor saw it, neither orientation could claim inherent precedence, natural or otherwise, as it had all, transparency and reflexive machinery and conscious and unconscious alike, flowed forth from the same font, much of said font fed by decades-deep, pedigree-prone MFA waters. The real issue right along, as Samuel Taylor saw it, was how to put good writing before readers who could appreciate good writing. Which put any self-respecting scribe in the ungainly position of trying to reach an increasingly indifferent readership, increasingly hooked on sensationalistic pap. And that predicament was as ideological as it was aesthetic, if no more so.

Tonight, at any rate, things were about to change, in ways neither writers nor storytellers could have imagined. When February hogs were up, Samuel Taylor knew only that he had grown weary of the accusations, the contentiousness, the divisiveness, all felt most acutely not by storytellers, but by writers. He decided that he didn't give a damn, finally, about the natural, or about denaturalizing it. However much esteem he might have garnered among his "self-conscious" peers, he was looking for a way out, or through. And he decided that, push come to shove, first and foremost, he wanted for a change to entertain.

Tonight, he wanted for a change to take some things for granted.

Tonight, he wanted for a change to tell stories.

Tonight, yes, it was memory, however faltering or precarious, that seemed to offer for Samuel Taylor's troubles at least the possibility of putting his ever receding but still accessible past to the service of telling said stories. It seemed a chance to make legible his subtler tenses, to tease out of himself not the nostalgic embrace, no, but the tried and true contours of a modestly storied past—it having been made abundantly evident thanks to the Web that *everyone's* past is storied—by employing only such fictive mucilage as was sufficient to sustaining the backward glance of an inquisitive expositor. Whatever artifice he might muster, whatever aperçus he might mobilize, events would be merely realigned, not recast outright.

Or such was the intention. He was aware that, in practice, the temptation to hybridize his screeds, to fabricate even among the most unalloyed of depositions, might prove overwhelming. But this would be storytelling, finally, not writing, thus would operate largely without the benefit of reflexive legerdemain to call attention to its deformations, albeit with no claim, for that matter, to unadulterated fact. So if liberties were to be taken, they had best be taken generically, under the aegis of fiction, thereby averting those stale controversies over implausibility and authenticity and the rest. Thus would something like an unconventional memoir become something like a conventional novel. And as for the unnamable, that battle cry of the besieged—among whose numbers he yet counted himself—it seemed to him that altogether too much had been made of trying to find a language for the languages endemic to the dark side of the street, a street that in recent years had been fashionably reimagined, whether dark side or bright, as Main Street USA. Of course transgression, like subversion, could be apropos; of course there should be no preset limit on subject matter; of course there would be writing that challenges orthodoxies of all sorts—but *fuck it* now seemed to Samuel Taylor the appropriate response to work that never rose above such thematics, such gymnastics, such dispensations.

Tonight, or so it had all seemed, even as it had seemed such a reactionary posture. And it had seemed also—as was alleged of Samuel Taylor by several of his peers in the years that followed—a chance for a change to put some jingle in his pocket.

Tonight, selling out? No. No shame tonight, thankyouverymuch.

Tonight, OK then, globalization.

*

Tonight, they'll be on their way back home. Up Old Liverpool Road, a left on Electronics Parkway. Then a right on Hopkins, a left on Buckley, a right on Shane, a left on—. Maybe a ten-minute drive in all, during which the two youngsters sit in the back of the Olds, preoccupied with the ordinary. With familiar territory.

Tonight, look at all those cars at the Randolph House.

Tonight, Mikey and his brother spot this guy—this body. This off-kilter body, hunched forward, hobbling along the shoulder of the Parkway, apparently in a hurry to go—to go where, exactly? Mikey and his brother point, excitedly, and make this bogey out to be a cripple—*The* Cripple. "It's The Cripple!" they exclaim together, laughing nervously, knowing it's wrong to laugh, but laughing anyhow.

Tonight, Vick Sr. is laughing too, not so much with his boys as at them. And Suzie—she's upset with the three of them. From that night on, Mikey and his brother keep an eye out for The Cripple.

*

Tonight, both writers and storytellers alike learn to develop an eye for the things that might interfere, the things that might get in the way. If they learn to strike while the iron is hot, they likewise learn when to interfere in the conflictual proceedings, and when not.

Tonight, it's like going to war, the storyteller might observe. You're merely exploiting an analogy, the writer might reply, adding that it's a dangerously jejune analogy to exploit.

Tonight, it's like going to war, avers the storyteller. Going to war is a last resort. Or should be, as a matter of principle. Practically speaking, if one waits *too* long to intervene in a conflict, or if one's interventions are ill-conceived, one might have an even more serious situation on one's hands. And we all know what happens with a world at war, says the storyteller. So our textual approach must be scrupulously planned, must not call attention to itself. A steady hand, low-key, nothing too irregular or obtrusive, lest we provoke the outbreak of hostilities. One must be, let us say, diplomatic.

Tonight, the writer wonders, And a text at war with itself? That can only be a metaphor, certainly, but taken figuratively, isn't it possible that a text at war with itself might be a desirable state of affairs, a way to push the stylistic envelope?

Tonight, imagine the loss when things go global, says the storyteller. Even the representation of war must not be warlike.

Tonight, imagine the narrative possibilities, says the writer. The representation of war ought to demonstrate, without remorse, that textual conflict is inexorable.

Tonight, Samuel Taylor imagines himself imagining a writer whose desire to become a storyteller, however much this might put him at war with himself, had him hanging up his jockstrap when February hogs were up.

*

Tonight, Vick watches as the old guy maneuvers his body into the car, his left leg bent at an odd angle. He struggles for a comfortable position, resting his right hand as a brace against the dashboard, sitting up and forward in his seat to make room for his left arm and hand behind him. He can see now that the old guy's left arm is fixed in this position—that it traces a tortuous, behind-the-back route, from the ball of his shoulder through this forearm, that ends with his left hand curled up and around, his fingertips reaching back toward his wrist. His fingernails are long, as much as an inch overgrown. No way could you get a glove on that hand.

Tonight, as he seats himself, the old guy turns to smile at Vick, managing only a half-turn and grin with only half his face.

Tonight, the old guy speaks rapidly, under his breath, running his thoughts together. The left side of his face contorts as he speaks, as if still frozen. He tries to get out as often as he can, *jogs* like this a couple of miles every night. Was in World War II, where he picked up *this*. Motions with his left shoulder-arm.

Tonight, Vick's father was in the war too.

Tonight, he picked up *this* there, in the battle, the battle of—

Tonight, he has two boys Vick's age.

Tonight, Vick can see that the old guy is smiling now, or half of his face is.

Tonight, Vick pulls over. The old guy opens the door, leaning against it and gripping it tightly with his right hand to pull himself up while twisting stiffly out of the bucket seat. It takes him a few seconds. Before he shuts the door, he nods his head back in, arm behind back, looking almost formal, dignified.

Tonight, *thank you, young fella.*

Tonight, as Vick pulls away, he can see the old guy in his side-view, jogging across the road behind him. It's two lanes each way, and it's dark, and patches of ice cover the road. But he can see that the old guy makes it across all right. He can also see, on the road ahead, a few slower moving vehicles. Vick knows how to handle a car on the ice, knows he has to slow down some as he comes up on these vehicles. He's surprised that so many people in these parts don't know when to slow down. It's as if they need a fender bender to remind them of where they are. Tonight, it's as if they can't remember, or don't want to.

End of story.

5 LAST NIGHT

Surely it was time someone invented a new plot, or that the author came out from the bushes.

Virginia Woolf

Last night, they're out there.

Last night, long-suffering coworkers with sulking profiles and pleading eyes, hoping against hope that there's a new payday under the sun.

Last night, he sits in a shabby little corridor reserved for doctoral students and adjunct faculty. Peering out through his office door, Samuel Taylor can see the door of the office across from his, and glued to the wall adjacent to this office is a 4" x 14" sign, white letters on black, that reads:

FICTION COLLECTIVE'S
MANUSCRIPT CENTRAL

Fiction Collective editorial having long since departed from said office—the famed small press publisher of unconventional fiction had in fact found a home on another state campus in another state, and after that, still another home—the sign serves to remind Samuel Taylor that academe, however glacial, is all about changing fortunes, greener pastures. Which, in light of his present circumstances, serves to give Samuel Taylor hope.

Last night, his small office has a window, and through this window Samuel Taylor has a nice view of the parking garage immediately adjacent to Stevenson—his building, named after the governor of Illinois who twice ran for president, and twice lost, on the Democratic ticket. Stevenson, the "egghead"—*that bastard Nixon*, Samuel

Taylor murmurs to himself, gazing out beyond the garage across the flat distances of the Land of Lincoln, the big March sky hovering silently above.

Last night, he's been busy chipping away on several pieces: a long poem, in prose, that he can't bring himself to call a prose poem; a screenplay on which he's collaborating with his wife, Nora; an autobiographical essay in six parts, "Illustrations to swallow up a thesis"; and a parable, he calls it, of academic life. He still hasn't decided on a title for the parable. He sits with his hands idle, wrists on his desk and fingers poised above the keyboard of his eight-year-old pink iMac. Some of his students make fun of the fact that his iMac is pink, but Samuel Taylor is piqued at their sense of humor, rooted as it is in a homophobic, rural code of masculinity—a masculinity he thought he'd left behind, at least in its more virulent forms, decades prior. He understands these kids better than they think, he thinks. They need to get over it.

Last night, he stares into the screen at a quote from Bishop Joseph Hall that serves as an epigraph to one piece:
'Mongst all these stirs of discontented strife,
O, let me lead an academic life;
To know much, and to think for nothing, know
Nothing to have, yet think we have enow.

Last night, in between classes, an orange ladybug will suddenly drift in front of his screen.

Last night, he'll reach for a tissue from the box on his desk, stand, and lean over to the wall adjacent to his desk to squish the ladybug—technically, the Multicolored Asian Lady Beetle, *Harmonia axyridis*—into the tissue. He'll toss the tissue in the wastebasket, absentmindedly sniffing his thumb and forefinger to see if the unmistakable odor of the bug has penetrated the tissue. It will have. He'll pump a blob of alcohol gel on his hands from the container on his desk, rub his palms and fingers together, and return to his seat, staring up at the crack above his window near the ceiling, out of which two more ladybugs will crawl even as he watches. He'll have to caulk that crack again, he'll think.

Last night, the ladybug infestation that plagues Stevenson and other campus buildings is the result of local farmers having imported the littler critters to eat aphids. Many on campus wonder whether, given the ecological consequences, importing non-native species really is preferable to using more pesticides—pesticides in use throughout the entire region at any rate, a reality of large-scale agribusiness— particularly in light of recent evidence to suggest that disintegrating ladybug carcasses are an allergen and might induce asthma.

Last night, Samuel Taylor has asthma. He considers whether he and the ladybugs share something in common, finally. Like the ladybugs, he's not a native of Illinois. But the ladybugs, by all accounts, are thriving, whereas he, by all accounts, is not. Perhaps he needs to get with the program, throw down some roots, convince his spouse—he has a tenure-track spouse, which makes him the "spousal accommodation"—that they're content, after all. Perhaps then they'll thrive here, in the Land of Lincoln, thinking they have enow.

Last night, ladybug, ladybug, fly away home.

Last night, he flicks a bug off his sweater with his middle finger, sending it sailing into the window casing, and stares back at the screen. Almost automatically, his fingers begin typing, all uppercase:
THIS
Then:
WAS
Pausing for a few seconds, he adds:
WRITTEN

Last night, one of his creative writing students will appear at his office door. Very cute, smiling. Nice kid, he'll think without thinking. Can't pace a story to save her life. But a nice kid. And at least she tries.

Last night, Jen sits on the green vinyl chair, angled toward Samuel Taylor. A ladybug lands on Samuel Taylor's copy of Abrams and Harpham's *A Glossary of Literary Terms* (eighth edition), which is lying open on his desk to page 145. Samuel Taylor eyes the dot of dotted orange with contempt as it migrates across the entry for "Ivory Tower" to take up ambulating residence at "Jeremiad." Flick, and Jen laughs.

Last night, he'll place Jen's creative nonfiction portfolio on his desk. A good ten minutes will pass while Samuel Taylor explains, cajoles, gestures with his hands, smiles, chuckles, digresses, inserts a four-letter word or two for effect, all of which will elicit nods of approval, along with the occasional request for clarification. Samuel Taylor is one good talker, has always had the gift of gab. He even manages to get in a plug for his forthcoming book without quite realizing that it's a plug. Jen is too green to be impressed, and too green not to be.

Last night, it's a happy meeting, and by the time the last trace of Jen's vanilla oil has wafted away, Samuel Taylor will have all but forgotten the details of what's transpired between them. He understands that Jen's writing will not change substantively as a result of their office interactions; for her writing to really work as literary art will require not semesters, but *years* of steady practice, and reading, and study. She'll need to cultivate a better bullshit detector, nurture a sensibility that knows *schwarmerei* when it sees it, learn how to apply the word *timbre* to her written compositions, and find it within herself to rein in the inevitable creative tics, or at least, to distribute them with greater consistency, something with which Samuel Taylor has himself so often struggled, so much of his work rejected as *rambling, uneven*—in the stinging words of his most perceptive detractor—*beset by a certain stubborn intelligence unduly enamored of aleatory and formal experiment.* This hit home, Samuel Taylor only too aware that his aversion to the discipline of conventional narrative had not a little to do with all those years he'd routinely, and at times begrudgingly, toed the line of a Fortune 500 engineering career. For him, writing had been an escape from such rigors, even if he had of late come to a renewed appreciation for the mechanics of story per se.

Last night, Samuel Taylor believes that Jen has it in her to become an OK writer, but he has no idea whether she has the enthusiasm and drive to spend years doing so, and her current employment prospects after graduation—her aunt needs help running a catering business on Chicago's South Side, and it's either that or an entry-level position with a publisher of board games—will likely provide little encouragement to pursue the writing life, especially given the brutal cultural emphases that attend eras of economic volatility such as the one in which Jen will make her way, and through which Samuel Taylor and his coworkers are presently struggling.

Last night, Samuel Taylor will wonder about the future of higher ed, *his* future in higher ed, and the future of writing itself. *What will happen if students like Jen elect to give up on writing and compose instead a video memoir, which is now being proposed as a curricular option? What if such video memoirs were to incorporate the kind of graphic material—violence, sexuality—that characterizes a goodly percentage of student writing? What if—*

Last night, Samuel Taylor will think, *What if Homo academicus, or economicus, or whatever, were to resolve to make do with imperfect bureaucratic trappings and look on the bright side for a change?* That's it—the bright side. Against rough beasts, sweetness and light. And sweetness and light *has* occasionally prevailed, hasn't it?—even in these gloomy, declension-ridden corridors. Even with perennially marginal academic writers like Samuel Taylor doling out their programmatic influence, their chestnuts of received wisdom, received from the Grandmamas and Grandpapas and Mamas and Papas of literature, to shape bundles of expressivity into variously Othered parcels of symbolic freight, some uncharacteristic few to be unpacked ages hence as symptomatic of something or other by Nike-clad supercomputing systems analysts or data miners or newer-age prophets, one could count on small doses of sweetness and light. Sweetness. And light.

Last night, and symbiosis? But weren't there systematic things that resisted systematized utterance? Didn't systems have outsides? Was this a *system*? Why not a clusterfuck of beginnings and endings and beginning-agains? Oh and why did the trade fiction market seem so woefully homogenized?

Last night, and what about beauty? *Great beauty causes great pain.* Not an apothegm, exactly, just his experience of the matter. Beauty, real beauty, beauty that mattered knocked him for a loop because it augured contact with some resonating fiber of all-is-one congruence. *We're all in this together*, from start to finish. Which was why he couldn't listen to Joni Mitchell every day, or gaze too frequently too closely for too long at Monet's Houses of Parliament series, or watch *La Strada* or *The Grapes of Wrath* every year, or reread *To the Lighthouse* more than once. Too much pain, too much selflessness, not enough difference, not enough alienation? Not quite.

Last night, and the ocean? And the mountains? He could look out over the sea, he would say, all the livelong day. Was this not beauty? Or was there something about natural beauty, the sublime, that "outrage on our imagination," as Kant had put it, that operated without regard for the human universe and its mortal needs?

Last night, here he was again, pretending to be a philosopher, and making a mess of things.

Last night, *wait*—was that right? He really could not gaze at a series of paintings? Two-dimensional spatial beauty had this effect on him too? And yet it wasn't the *punctum* that wounded him while examining the old black and white photo of his brother and him as kids standing beside a small evergreen that would eventually grow to such a height that the new owners of the family home, sold after the divorce, would ultimately have to have it cut down. It wasn't the image—not the quality of the image, not the nostalgia such images typically convey. It was the *intention* behind the image—the father or, far more likely, mother who'd wished to preserve that image, while scaling human growth to pine. The intention, yes, that was it. Even when his sentimental conjurings had been reflected back at him with that "certain alienated majesty" of which Emerson had written—with regard to works of genius, to be true—a consciousness capable of selecting and developing material for preservation and future reference, if not reverence, was marked by its intention. And with this realization he had long since become aware of his limitations as a would-be maker of literary art. No point in trying to rationalize it into a virtue. Notwithstanding his avant sympathies, there it was.

Last night, he takes a deep breath, and looks down at his watch. He picks up a few books for class, and his CamelBak, and heads out the door, oddly emboldened.

*

Last night, a visit to the periodontist to check on Samuel Taylor's ever-receding gums. The hygienist has just finished cleaning his teeth, and he now waits for the perio to look things over, passing the time by reading the labels on the equipment—*Pelton & Crane,* an embossed cursive—and the diplomas on the wall. His seat is reclined backward, pitching Samuel Taylor's face toward the ceiling, so he has to raise his head a bit to read the fine print on the diplomas. Samuel Taylor, who himself holds a doctorate, notes that the perio has graduated from more prestigious—higher tier, as they call it in the trade—institutions than has he. This fact reassures Samuel Taylor—he wouldn't want some bottom-tier clown picking at his gums, right?—while opening an old wound having to do with why he hadn't himself attended a top-tier school. The reason was quite simple: he'd never given it any serious thought, hailing as he did from the working- and under-classes. He didn't even know back then that there *were* tiers.

Last night, OK, that might be something of a dodge. So his ignorance is his fault and his alone.

Last night, the perio is a cordial if slightly brusque man, perhaps a few years older than his patient, but nearly bald. Samuel Taylor considers whether he would swap his pocketed gums and full crop of hair for the perio's perfect smile and receding hairline.

Last night, no.

Last night, the perio strikes you as one of those guys who always knew what he wanted to be, and how his life would turn out. And Samuel Taylor suspects that the perio's life is in fact turning out exactly as he knew it would. Most important, thinks Samuel Taylor, if your gums need to be cut open, he's the kind of guy you want to cut open your gums. He doubts himself and his profession not a whit, and his profession has rewarded him, and by all accounts, rewarded him handsomely, for this failure to doubt. He comes highly recommended, Samuel Taylor having been sent there by referral from his third-generation dentist.

Last night
>   How're you doing, Doc?
>   Quite well, thank you Samuel.
>   The two men exchange firm handshakes.
>   Let's have a look.

Last night, Samuel Taylor opens wide as the perio pokes around inside with a metal probe.

Last night
>   That hurt?
>   Nuh.
>   How's teaching going?
>   Guh.
>   What are you teaching again?

Last night, the perio pauses for a moment, withdrawing the probe to allow his patient to answer: literature, and creative writing.

Last night, the perio reinserts the probe, occasionally poking a gum hard enough to remind Samuel Taylor that he's entirely at the mercy of the perio's skill level. Samuel Taylor recalls the diplomas on the wall.

Last night, a few moments pass.

Last night
    Creative writing, huh?
    Yuh.
    The perio continues with his probe.
    You can't really teach that, can you?
    Ell—

Last night, Samuel Taylor ventures something of an open-mouthed smile, which, under the circumstances, contorts into a grimace. The perio keeps probing, and checking, and probing.

Last night
    I say you can't really teach that, can you?

Last night, Samuel Taylor falls off into a sort of reverie.

Last night, suddenly Samuel Taylor raises his right hand to grip the perio's wrist firmly, pulling back the perio's hand to extract the probe from his mouth. He takes a deep breath.

Last night, an eternity passes while Samuel Taylor considers how best to respond: whether to regale the Doc with the history of creative writing and corresponding misconceptions as to creativity and craft and the like, misconceptions with which one must contend on a regular basis; whether to inform the Doc that he finds it unfortunate that a medical professional of his stature should feel free to suggest to a patient that the patient's profession requires little in the way of expertise, the less than subtle implication being that the dental profession is marked by its practitioners' skillful application of a body of knowledge; whether even to ask the Doc whether he's ever tried to write a poem or a story; or whether simply to snap the Doc's wrist back hard so as to jam the probe into his fat fucking overfed, and unduly complacent, face.

Last night, what a video that would make.

Last night
    Samuel?
    Yeah?
    Samuel—you OK?
    Yeah. Yeah Doc, sorry. Drifted off for a bit there. Long day.
    You're all set, Samuel. Gums look great—keep it up.
    Thanks Doc.

*

THIS WAS WRITTEN

This was written while en route to Paris to meet my friend and mentor, Gilbert Vindefou, a long-time resident of the Onzième with whom I studied Baudelaire and share a particular fondness, really more of an affliction, for éclairs served with Lillet on the rocks and a twist of lime, the Brasserie Lipp garçon instructed to stand at the ready with Alka-Seltzer tablets and a jigger of Pepto-Bismol.

This was written after reading some really bad poetry and thinking, *Hell—I can do that.*

This was written while traveling along my mother's birth canal wondering whether the glint of an instrument at the end of the passageway was in fact a pair of spade forceps and thus somewhat anxious that upon my emergence I would be tossed into a killing jar, pinned through the thorax to a mounting board, set in a glass frame, and placed on sale forever at a high-end gift shop in East Bumblefuck, PA.

This was written on the same day that Araki Yasusada and Girly Man were in Massachusetts together applying for a marriage license.

This was written while pondering whether it's the artist's place to find ways of addressing human suffering in, say, Iraq, Iran, Palestine, Afghanistan, North Korea, Sudan, Mexico, and Detroit, and as this sentence hurtled toward its conclusion, it occurred to me that my mind had drifted, as, lamentably, human minds are prone to, in my case to settle upon the éclair that the garçon had been kind enough to place right under my nose.

This was written under the influence of an éclair, while trying to write popular fiction. Which is to say, this was written while trying to entertain *myself.*

This was written immediately after eating the largest pussy I've ever had the pleasure of bringing to orgasm, so large in fact that propped up inside was a 37″ flat screen on which Eileen Myles was demonstrating the proper way to eat pussy, a lesson—believe me when I say—in restraint.

This was written to remind you that dessert has been served more than once already, so you might be wearing out your welcome.

This was written with the understanding that if you see war where I see peace, if you see hate where I see love, if you see sorrow where I see happiness, well then: either the two of us together make one goddamn great philosopher, or maybe we should write a pop song together?

This was written while observing that immature poets imitate, mature poets ripen, then rot.

This was written to assure you that while we all may need the applause, it might be a good idea if you were to stop publishing anthologies filled with work by your friends; and *then* creating an aesthetic rationale for their inclusion.

This was written to inform all you entitled little shits out there—and if you don't know who you are, then your parents know who you are, unless your parents are themselves entitled little shits, in which event this was written to inform an entire population of dumbshits—that if you think buying something is tantamount to knowing about something, and if you think knowing about something is tantamount to knowing how to do something, and if you think knowing how to do something is tantamount to knowing how to do something well, and if you think knowing how to do something well is tantamount to doing something well, and if you think doing something well is tantamount to doing something actually worth doing, then you're nothing but entitled little shits.

And as a codicil to this last, this was written while sitting at home in front of my computer, gazing out the window at the basketball backboard that my next-door neighbor Abe has decided to put up for his kids, and which now serves as a magnet for all of the neighborhood kids, and which appears a sociable enough gesture on Abe's part, but which is in actuality part of a recruiting strategy of a North Carolina sports ministry, Upward, that has doubtless assured Abe a ticket to a happy hereafter if he ferrets out rebounding converts, even though Abe—or "Abel," as he likes to refer to himself—has tried to legislate parking restrictions for the rest of us while parking his son's car and his wife's SUV and assorted trailers at his end of the street and while roaring back and forth to work, one mile away, in the largest pickup this side of Sarah Palin Land, has assaulted my next-door neighbor to the west with a baseball bat, and has, I regret to report, pushed me on one occasion to the brink of fisticuffs with the entire neighborhood looking on. And to make matters worse, Abe's employer is my employer. All of which is to say that this was written in a state of dismay: dismayed at Mayor Abe, dismayed at sports ministries, dismayed in particular at the sight of Abe's eight-year-old shooting hoop alone even in freezing weather, the basket lowered to accommodate his height, a short boy even for his age and, in light of his father's example and to judge by how he interacts with his peers, bound to develop over time some mild form of assholiness, the runt out there day after day after day, the basketball bouncing and bouncing and bouncing, me gazing out the window wanting to like the kid, wanting even to like Abe, wanting at least not to dislike Abe, wanting at least not to want to kick Abe's ass up and down the street, but dismayed in any case at the notion that the obsessive pursuit of basketball basketball basketball, or poetry poetry poetry, really can, all by its lonesome, lift you off the ground.

Maybe true. Maybe not true. Better you believe.

Old Sherpa saying

He's probably aiding—looks like he's hanging from his pro. They're both sitting in the Blazer, gazing up through the wind- shield, an unusually warm day in early March. The creek is a tor- rent of runoff—snowmelt, along with some unknown proportion of glacier melt—and the sun is sharp even this early in the year. At this bend in the access road, though, the canyon is shading the rock. They angle their heads up to see how he's doing. Is that a difficult route? Pretty difficult. Maybe 5.11b. There's a technique for everything, and an associated vocabu- lary, and in this case, a numbered ranking. Thanks to Nora, Samuel Taylor hikes quite a bit, and so he knows his way around a noun like *talus*—as in, *That fucking talus on Quandary tore the shit out of my big toe*—and a phrasal verb like *peak out*—as in, *Couldn't peak out on Annapurna III, ran low on food*—and an acronym like *MFA*—as in, *5.9 my fucking ass*. But he knows nothing about rock climbing first-hand, and what he does know he's learned through direct ob- servation, and hanging around members of the Boulder climbing community, and reading the climbing magazines his brother Mike tosses Nora's way. So when Mike says to his rock-climbing buddies, over a few beers at the Sun later that day, *So close to the rock, you could belay right out of the car*, and then mentions a photo taken of him in Mexico, at El Potrero Chico, doing just that, the joke is not entirely lost on Samuel Taylor. But neither is he at one with the laughter.

Later that evening, after a manic drive back down the canyon in Mike's Blazer with Mike screaming through the windshield at the abysmally slow traffic, Samuel Taylor prepares his Linguine alla Vit- torio for Nora, Mike, and Mike's German girlfriend, Christa. (Nora bakes the bread.) Everyone agrees—it's a great dish. Samuel Taylor insists that anyone can make it.

*

It's 7 a.m. on a Monday morning, and Vick is hitting crosstown traffic on his ten-speed. He's a little apprehensive about the job. But he needs summer work to make it through his master's degree, his a-little-bit-late-in-life graduate studies. In English. In language and its many uses.

He rides into the Grimm's lot, and stows the bike in his customary spot around the back of one of the storage buildings. Manny, the foreman, is always there early—it's a Teamster shop, but he's already learned that it's not what most people think of when they think union labor.

Hey Vick, how ya doin?

Pretty good Manny.

Beautiful day.

Yeah.

You like that bike a yours?

It's OK. Gotta watch the traffic though.

Real assholes on the road these days, right? Hey—didn't you bring lunch?

Kinda forgot. Figured I'd pick something up at that grocer on the other side of the underpass.

Don't worry about it—I gotta coupla baloney sandwiches. You can have one.

I don't wanna take your food, Manny.

Don't worry about it Vick. My wife makes 'em for me. They're good.

Manny tells Vick to head over to the rock pile and start filling some bags. They've got to deliver fifty bags of stone before noon to a contractor on the outskirts of town. He'll be helping Robert, one of the regular drivers.

He grabs a shovel and an armful of bags, and walks over to the pile of #2 and #3 washed stone. It's already hot and humid. He fills the bag carefully with a few shovelfuls until it can stand open by itself. Then he digs into the work, filling a bag every four or five minutes, tying it with some twine, lifting it knee-high and swinging it out of the way. When full, a bag of stone weighs between 100 and 120 lbs. He ties up a half dozen bags by the time Robert walks up.

Hey.

Hey.

Gonna be a scorcher.

Yeah. If it don't rain.

Get any shoots in over the weekend?

Did a wedding.

A wedding! How'd it go?

Went pretty well, I think.

Cool.

You been giving any thought to my offer?

I think I'm gonna hang onto it.

Well if you change your mind, I could use another good 35.

I'll keep it in mind.

It takes them the better part of an hour to finish filling all fifty bags, after which they have to load them onto a flatbed for delivery. Vick hops in the passenger's side, and Robert drives.

Manny's gonna give me one of his baloney sandwiches for lunch. He's a gem, that guy.

Robert doesn't reply.

Got an odd idea of what bull-work is though.

What do you mean?

Well he keeps telling me there's no bull-work around here.

What the fuck do you call what we're doing right now?

That's what I'm saying.

Manny's OK, but I wish he'd stop talking that shit. Problem with the guy is that he's been busting his ass for so long he doesn't know anymore when it's being busted.

By the time they arrive at the contractor's, a thunderstorm has moved in and moved out. The entranceway slopes down and under a roof canopy that extends out from the contractor's garage in front of a makeshift loading dock area—for pickup trucks. Robert is not happy.

Who's the jerkoff who devised this abortion.

Robert backs up carefully as far as he can go. The tail end of the flatbed rests under the overhang, not enough room for a man to stand. The contractor wants them to drop the bags onto the loading dock. It's still sprinkling, and the bags are soaked. This means you have to pick up a bag, walk it over to the overhang, duck down, then hump it for six feet bent half over until you can drop it onto the concrete floor of the dock.

In the rain.

Twice that day Vick almost fucks himself up but good, once nearly slipping and installing his face on the gutter along the overhang, the other time nearly sliding below it and dropping the bag of rocks onto his chest.

Robert laughs as they drive off.

No bull-work my ass. This chickenshit outfit doesn't even own a truck with a winch. Whoever heard of a building supply company without a winch?

As they pull into Grimm's, the clouds have lifted and the sun is out again. Robert parks the truck in the far corner of the lot and they begin their ten o'clock break by resting their arms out the window and talking about the fucked-up weather. The air so heavy now with water vapor that their motionless forearms bead sweat.

I'm parched.

Me too.

They get out of the truck and walk up a slight grade to the larger of two storage buildings, where Grimm's warehouses most of the bagged cement mix on pallets. Manny greets them at the overhead door, which overlooks the lot.

How'd it go?

Not bad.

New guy here hold up OK?

Robert smiles.

He did OK.

Thanks a lot fellas.

There's a hose hooked up to a spigot in the corner of the storage building. Robert and Vick help themselves, and as they do so, a supply truck pulls into the lot. Manny's eyes glare the moment he sees it, and he shakes his head.

Those cocksuckers.

Robert rolls his eyes.

Robert, why'nt you give Marty and the Retard a hand with that brick load. Vick and I will tackle these cocksuckers.

For his part, Vick has no idea what Manny is so worked up about.

*

This never happened, but it's true, every word of it. Party of three:

Let me put it this way: do you remember what Dirty Harry says in *Magnum Force?*

A man's got to realize—

Got to *know*—

His limitations. That's right. That about sums it up.

What are you trying to tell us?

It just seems to me that you people keep circling back to the same issue.

Which is—?

Who puts the most on the line. Who can take the most punishment. Who's the most extreme. Who's the best hung, the most tumescent, whatever. It's all the same thing.

What's your point? People do what they do.

Did he say *tumescent?*

That's right Godard, tumescent. Look it up. And people just don't come out of the womb doing what they do. There are cultural factors—

Bullshit.

There are cultural factors that influence what we do. Why people should end up doing things they probably shouldn't be doing is one thing.

Who are you to say?

It's up to each person. I'd insist only that each person cultivate the ability to scrutinize his or her actions.

How do you know they don't?

I can't be certain, but the discussion only gets interesting when we're willing to speculate about such things. Look, my real issue isn't whether—

Bait and switch.

Bait and switch my ass. My real issue isn't whether you want to kill yourself running down a trail or jumping off a building—

Where's your sense of adventure?

Can I speak?

You've been doing all the talking.

My real issue is how such activities connect with everything else in the world. Talking with you people I sometimes get the impression that there *isn't* anything else in the world.

So you find our climbing discussions boring, is that it?

Fuck yeah, sometimes. About as boring as harping on about some obscure literary text.

What do *you* wanna talk about?

I just think there are times we should be talking about something other than our own immediate interests.

Like what?

Like lots of things. The news.

I don't need to know about the local news.

I'm not talking about the local news. For that matter, what does it mean to say that you don't need to know about the local news?

What's wrong with discussing our passions?—what makes us happy.

You can be passionate about apple pie, arson, or anal sex. I'd be happy to discuss any of these, but if any of these dominated the discussion, I'd be worried about us.

Even anal sex?

OK, we'll make an exception for anal sex.

Whatever floats your boat, is what I say.

That's what you say. I'm just saying there are things more important than our appetites.

Like what?

Do I really have to answer that question?

Yeah, you do.

*

Of late Samuel Taylor has found himself hanging by his metaphors. He's positively stoked after a boulder traverse, and gearing up for the couloir. After a grody approach, he's dying to toke up, but figures he'll wait till after they bivy. He's under a flake along the dihedral, at the crux of a chossy route and about to sprong, when his manky tricam pops out an inch. He bags two peaks before he biffs it and trashes his knee, and *then* the gropple starts to come down. He's campused so much he barely has the strength for the rap down—

Actually, no. He's no climber. His thoughts have simply wandered off during dinner one evening at a popular Mexican restaurant, where he's learned that he and the other three men seated at the table are mechanical engineers. The other three men are climbers, as are three of the women. Samuel Taylor's mind is working overtime to relate to the climbing risks these men and women seem to enjoy. But he's finding it difficult to relate both to the specific risks entailed and to the way risk as such is discussed by these men, these former engineers. To add to which, Samuel Taylor has noticed how thoroughly talk of climbing dominates the conversation, the athletic ferment of this former Front Range village, now city, eschewing any but a cursory concern for the global village and its tribulations. Too often he and Nora are left with very little to do but to ask questions, and rarely are their questions returned in kind.

So while Samuel Taylor and Nora sit silently, sipping their margaritas, bumping knees under the table, Samuel Taylor's brother gives them to understand, in so many words, that risk is minimal, that in fact the climber controls the climb, because if you know what you're doing, and you're careful, and your gear is in good shape, you shouldn't have any problems.

Samuel Taylor nods.

Safety is built into the sport in an important sense, Mike explains, from the equipment required up-front to the path most follow in becoming climbers. You start with relatively easy climbs, under the watchful eye of an experienced climber, and you progress to more difficult climbs, accompanied by a guide like Mike.

Samuel Taylor nods.

If you learn good safety habits from the start, and if you keep your wits about you and practice Right Thinking, Mike asserts, these will take care of you throughout your climbing life.

Samuel Taylor nods, mulling over the construction *climbing life*. Mike continues.

But Samuel Taylor is stuck at *climbing life*. And your *writing life*, he thinks, the life of the mind? What sort of construction is that?

Samuel Taylor is about to lead a climb up a bolted slab—a slab that's already been *freed*, as they say. He climbs up on belay—Mike is below, spotting him—and he uses his hands and feet to support himself between bolts. At each bolt he clips in with a beener. If he falls, Samuel Taylor assures himself, he'll fall at most only the distance between two bolts, because Mike knows what he's doing. Still, if he falls, the edge of that rock over there is not the place to—

Actually, no. He's no climber. Based on what Samuel Taylor has been able to glean from talking to his brother and his climbing friends, there's a stubborn libertarian streak at the core of most climbers, to which Samuel Taylor can at some level relate, having had his own share of mind-numbing encounters with organizational ineptitude. But gravity will never relent, as he sees it, and rock will never reform. So it seems to Samuel Taylor that climbing is an activity in which one ought never to underestimate the relentless and unreformed nature of the competition, one's political convictions notwithstanding.

This is Samuel Taylor in the summer. This is Samuel Taylor's summer. Now that he holds a doctorate. Now that he's a professor, but no climber.

*

Manny guides the supply truck as it backs up to the overhead door. The truck bed is loaded down with four pallets of what look to be smallish, foot-square boxes. When the back of the truck bed reaches the door, Manny whistles to the driver to stop, and hops on a forklift parked near the rear of the storage building. In a few minutes he's unloaded the four pallets and the driver is on his way. He reaches for a pair of snips and cuts the bands securing the boxes to the pallet.

What have we got here?

Cocksuckers, Vick. Pick one up.

Vick walks over, grabs one of the boxes on top with his right hand, and pulls. The box barely budges.

What'd I tell ya, Vick—cocksuckers.

Vick pulls a bit harder, tightening his gut for the load when it drops off the pallet into his hands. The load drops all right—about fifty pounds' worth falls up against his chest. He rests it on the cement floor.

What's inside these things?

Open one up. Here—

Manny reaches into his trouser pocket and tosses Vick his jackknife. Vick scores the tape seal, pries open the cardboard top to reveal spools of wire. Each box is crammed tight with spools of solid-core wire.

Jesus Fuck.

Yeah, and you should see where we gotta put these cocksuckers. C'mon.

Manny bends, folds the cocksucker's cardboard flaps shut and scoops it up, resting it with a little effort on the right shoulder of his sixty-year-old frame. Vick follows him toward the back of the storage building, which is lined with heavy steel racks. It's a dirty, dingy old place that probably hasn't seen many changes in the past two or three decades. Manny points to the bottom tier of one set of racks.

They gotta go down there.

He bends down, sliding the cocksucker off his shoulder and cradling it in his right arm as he gets on all fours and crawls under the bottommost shelf to muscle the cocksucker up against the back wall, where they'll begin stacking them. Manny's baseball cap catches the top of the shelf as he crawls back out, and Vick watches as Manny stands, uncurling his aging frame, straightening his cap, dusting off his trousers. The thought occurs to Vick that this is perhaps the worst place in the entire Grimm's facility to store cocksuckers—but he keeps it to himself, not having been working here long enough to earn a say in how things are done. The thought occurs to Vick that there should be an applied science pertinent to the unloading and stacking of cocksuckers, with the aim of improving efficiency and safety, but he keeps it to himself, not having been working here even the month required to qualify for a union card. The thought occurs to Vick, the same thought that occurred to him a decade prior, that this is not how he wants to spend his act three, but he keeps it to himself.

So they get to it, using a hand truck to bring six cocksuckers at a time to their final resting place. Thing is, every working surface of Manny's body is covered over with calluses, whereas Vick—his olive-smooth skin is taking a real beating whenever the cardboard cocksuckers rub up against it, which they do each time he crouches down to cradle them. He's ending up with cardboard burns on his chest, stomach and the insides of his forearms. The cocksuckers are wrecking him.

*

Samuel Taylor and Nora hike together. They get out of bed at 4 a.m. to be at the trail head by 6 a.m. so that they can be down before the storms roll in at 2 p.m. Mike likes to climb with his friends. He gets out of bed at 4 a.m. to be at the trail head to start the approach by 6 a.m. so that he can begin the first pitch by 9 a.m. and be down before the storms roll in at 2 p.m. There's a lot to these sports, and because of the commitment of time, energy, and resources, it's not unusual to spend one's free time with other like-minded individuals. And while Samuel Taylor and Nora are, technically, outsiders as far as the climbing community goes—hikers ranked decidedly lower than climbers in the risk-taking, thrill-seeking pecking order—the fact that Samuel Taylor is Mike's brother gives him and his wife entrée into this community. Having spent considerable time with climbers, husband and wife have come to enjoy their company—these are good people, by and large, with no shortage of the decency and generosity you find in all walks of life. But Samuel Taylor is beginning to suspect that too many of these people climb in order to compensate for their salaried lives—they seek a degree of modulated autonomy and empowerment rarely available at their jobs, as most of these people seem but to suffer their jobs—and that a control freak ethos lurks behind too many of their utterances, too many of which register only the narrow aspirations of climbing. And Samuel Taylor is no climber.

He's noted a tendency in particular to venerate those daredevil types who, even by climbers' precipitous standards, perform death-defying, parkour-like feats, and manage miraculously to survive, albeit often with the subsequent aid of dozens of stitches, staples and pins—and, in the high-elevation climbing world, sherpas. Danger seduces us all, to varying degrees. But if gear plus technique plus attitude equals control, the greatest climbers, following this line of thinking, are nonetheless those willing to push themselves to the threshold of what gear can safely provide.

Samuel Taylor has noted too that if climbers tend as a group to resent the conjecture that death lies in wait, they yet relate mightily to any discussion of the body and its ailments. Climbing is tough on the body, and most of the climbers he meets supplement their climbing activities with regular trips to the gym, yoga classes, off-season sports like skiing or orienteering, what have you. They're much like dancers or bodybuilders, he's observed, in that they preen over their bodies—in this case, their thick forearms, sausage fingers, and remarkably low body fat. And they all, without exception, suffer regular physical injury as a result of climbing: tendonitis, torn ACL or MCL, evulsion fracture, torn bicep, you name it. Physical therapy, massage, and acupuncture are routine maintenance operations in this community, supplemented by every painkiller and herbal remedy imaginable. This is a high-maintenance activity, and despite the brainy application of brawn, it produces high-maintenance subjects.

And truth be told, this orientation toward the ever-reparable, ruggedly assembled body-machine, and the hermetic discourse that surrounds it, is beginning to wear a bit thin on Samuel Taylor, whose doctoral dissertation had, after all, to do with the notion of the self-made engineer in the postwar world. He has, after all, led the writing life, the life of the mind, for upwards of two decades now.

The writing life.

Don't you hear yourselves? Aren't you hip technicians attuned to the flighty New Age inflections of your rock-warrior élan? Is it entirely lost on you that the language of sports psychology conceals your more narcissistic impulses? Do you really think you *thought* your way to the summit? Teleportation, anyone? Have you *thought* your way to the implications of your DIY, self-help outlook? Of course the mind has a great deal to do with one's well-being. But if all the Right Thinking in the world can't seem to cure a person's suffering, it can certainly put the onus on the person who suffers, right?—who evidently hasn't thought positively *enough*. This would include the poor, yes? In fact, where *is* the suborned Other in all of this? Reduced to Sasquatch or Yeti status? Animal consciousness? Rocks and minerals and lichen—

Is this what you call *living the dream?*

Ah, Samuel Taylor thinks, the writing life, the life of the mind. The leisure to write summers, and to discover what he thinks, all thanks to his job, his position. With tenure, he'll be set. *They'll* be set, he and Nora. With tenure.

*

Manny and Vick wrestle with the cocksuckers till noon, at which point, covered head to toe with dirt and grime and cobwebs and sweat—the older man's mustache, like the younger man's beard, caked with dust—Vick takes Manny up on that baloney sandwich, not having the energy to bike down the road and back. They rinse off in the restroom toward the back of the storage building, and walk over to the small office building to buy a Coke from the machine there. The office staff never fails to greet their appearance with the same combination of disdain and indifference. Manny doesn't make eye contact, never says a word.

They meet Robert, Marty and Adam—whom the men refer to with equal parts mischief and scorn as the Retard—back at the cement pallets. They sit on the bags while they chow down, puffs of cement dust filtering through the seams as they shift in their seats, the air dense with a dusty haze.

Vick bites into the sandwich. This is a good baloney sandwich, a goddamn good baloney sandwich, he thinks to himself. In fact it's a great baloney sandwich, he thinks, just the right amount of dark mustard, and provolone, and top-shelf baloney, on fresh Italian bread. With another bite, it occurs to Vick that this just might be the best fucking baloney sandwich he's ever eaten. With half a dill pickle, no less.

Manny, do me a favor and tell your wife she makes a great fucking baloney sandwich.

He wolfs the sandwich down as Manny and Marty smile the same knowing smile. Marty is a guy about Vick's age, but leaner, fitter. He's been doing this for six years now. Vick can't quite get a fix on Marty.

Evidently he once owned three thousand jazz and blues albums, but for some reason decided to sell them all.

Why'd you do that?

Marty shrugs his shoulders.

Don't know. Just got sick of it, I guess.

Adam, the Retard, eyes Vick with suspicion. He doesn't like Vick. He thinks Vick is trying to steal his job. He's been working at Grimm's for two years, is a big, strapping, slow-on-the-uptake guy in his early twenties who doesn't remotely comprehend what it means to work summers in between semesters, anymore than Vick comprehends what it means to aspire to a permanent job at Grimm's. Adam never finished high school. And he's married. And he has a kid. He tells Vick one time about how he puts pepper in his kid's mouth to stop him from acting up.

Pepper? Think that's gonna work?

Worked when my parents did it to me. Ain't gonna listen to no brat.

*

What are you, some kinda pussy?

That's right, that's what I am—a pussy.

These two guys have been at it now for better than an hour, over two pitchers of Kind Ale, and Samuel Taylor can tell that the older guy is struggling to maintain his sense of humor. In between eavesdropping, Samuel Taylor has begun brooding over the logic of calculated risks. He's starting to understand said logic as predicated on an unwillingness to examine closely the calculus of risk and its associated motivations—a bigger picture in which the most superbly conditioned athlete, aided by the most expertly crafted gear, wages an improvised battle under the sun against the permanence of gravity and rock and the shifting nature of circumstance.

C'mon—it's a girlfriend 5.8, if that.

I told you—my elbow is still killing me.

Samuel Taylor recalls Emerson, his laundry list of items that mark a successful life. Emerson had included "leav[ing] the world a bit better, whether by a healthy child, a garden patch or a redeemed social condition" and "to know even one life has breathed easier because you have lived." It's possible that times have changed, thinks Samuel Taylor, and that nobody today can reasonably imagine contributing to the spirit of such a list—namely, to contribute to a better world.

Hell, Sheila's going. And if Sheila can top-rope it, anyone can.

Wait till *you're* fifty, bud, see how fast *you* heal.

It's possible that the way people talk about their lives has little to do with how they actually live their lives, thinks Samuel Taylor, and how they think about the world.

Fucking old man crying in his beer.

That's right, that's what I am—an old man. A pussified old man. At least I can still eat pussy.

It's possible that climbing discourse is but an extension and intensification of that narrow-minded brand of pragmatism that punctuates US public discourse generally, thinks Samuel Taylor, in which the art object itself is often seen through the lens of investment analysis.

I got the next 'round.

Fuck you—I got it.

And it's possible, too, that climbers simply bond over climbing, and that Samuel Taylor is just envious. After all, he concedes, these people have guts.

OK—so he *is* envious.

Still, he thinks, *something* must account for this studied conversational neglect, this self-absorption underwriting climbing discourse, where so much that is intimately human is excluded in order to give the manageable its due. It strikes Samuel Taylor that for all of the talk of freeing the rock and liberating the bureaucratized self, even discourse itself must be controlled. And isn't engineering all about control?

But it's the same with physicists. Plumbers. And poets—who ply their trade at times with humorless intensity, and whose oracular testimony proves a bit too much at times even for Samuel Taylor's vatic hankerings. *Any* professionalized discourse, it seems, whether operating under the sign of climbing, engineering, or writing, can evidently turn in on itself, and neglect its outsides. Its givens.

Elbow shmelbow. You seem to be swinging the brews OK, so why baby that thing? You could sit on your ass all day and it'd still be fucked-up.

Got that right. So think of me sitting on my ass all day and getting fucked-up. They're calling for high winds tomorrow anyway.

Samuel Taylor suddenly realizes that he craves talk of what's been happening in Palestine. New Orleans. Afghanistan. Down the street at Moe's. His yearnings couldn't be further removed from climbing and its vicissitudes, or, for that matter, from those other fast-forward obsessions of the upwardly mobile in these precincts, foremost among which are Rocky Mountain weather and Boulder real estate.

This is Samuel Taylor in the summer. This is Samuel Taylor's summer, in Boulder, where he's no climber.

He looks around the bar, taking note of its bustling wait staff and its affluent, noisy patrons. Gazing beyond the interior, through the windows facing east, he beholds now the brown haze that hovers above the high plains at this time of day. Everything seems at once and forever to take on a new urgency. We need to de-optimize, he thinks, even as we specialize. Or better, we need to understand our strivings toward functional effectiveness and the discourses that embody such strivings as but one aspect of our larger, longer-term needs, needs that require attention as well to intellectual or affective or spiritual ends, ends that cannot always be readily quantified and assessed. And we don't have much time.

Or so does Samuel Taylor conclude, based on his fieldwork.

*

They've been sitting for twenty minutes making small talk—Vick trying in vain to get a discussion going about Chernobyl, or the election of Waldheim as president of Austria, or Hands Across America, and having finally to settle for the Yankees's shot at a pennant—when the second of Grimm's flatbeds pulls into the lot. It's Lester, back from a brick delivery. Bricks and cement are Grimm's meat and potatoes.

Manny scowls as Lester walks into the building, speaking just loud enough for Lester to hear what he's saying.

There goes the neighborhood.

Lester pretends to size up his coworkers.

Some neighborhood.

Manny is not crazy about Lester. Nobody is. Lester is pushing fifty, gives the first and last impression of being something of a slob along with something of a know-it-all. Slob: by his own account, Lester got so drunk one night that he threw up his partial. Thing is, he never bothered to replace it. Know-it-all: during the entire time that Vick knows Lester, he's on a diet, and will lecture anyone willing to listen on the number of calories in a grape or a peach or a piece of pie. This coming from an unshaven man with a toothless grin and a stained tee stretched tight around a beer belly that enters the room a second before he does.

Though Manny has seniority and is the man in charge, he and Lester share casual authority as the elders of Grimm's tiny workforce. And though Lester may not look the part, under all that beer fat is a body that can work hard, push come to shove.

A few days prior, Vick had helped Lester with a residential brick delivery. Lester loaded the pallets of bricks on the flatbed using the forklift, but because Grimm's has no winch truck—technically, a truck having a winch-operated crane—all the bricks would have to be unloaded manually.

It's another hot day. They arrive at the country residence at 9 a.m. and are greeted by a neatly dressed woman in her fifties who has that unassuming air about her that one associates with rural life. She explains that her husband, a vet, has been called away to an emergency, but that she knows where he wants them to deposit the bricks. Lester and Vick get started. Using a brick tong, Lester grabs six or eight of the red rectangles from the pallet, placing them on the flatbed, and Vick uses an identical tong to grab the six or eight bricks and stack them on the ground. A half-hour into it and Vick can sense the rhythm that their two bodies have begun to establish, each with the other. Vick doesn't really care for Lester, and he doubts that Lester really cares for him, but they're nonetheless bonding over the job before them. Over work, a temporary glue.

After a couple of hours, the woman comes out to offer them lemonade. Lester being Lester, he doesn't hesitate to accept. But he is, in truth, polite about it, and there's no rule in that corner of the home delivery world against accepting kindness from customers. Or, there wasn't then.

They've been sitting on the pallets now for upwards of forty-five minutes.

OK guys, back to work. Vick, we got a guy coming in, needs forty bags of cement. Can you handle that?

No sweat, Manny.

Picking up an eighty-pound bag of cement is not that difficult once you get the hang of it, and requires less sheer strength than co-ordination and balance. If you're high on the pallet you can get your shoulder into the bag. If you're low, you have to bend a bit, which means squaring your shoulders and getting your legs into it. Vick has seen the strongest guys topple backwards once the bag folds and the weight inside shifts a bit.

As with everything else, practice makes perfect. And Vick was getting plenty of practice at Grimm's.

*

Mike had an accident a year ago. He fell—on belay of course—while trying to reach a difficult hold. He dropped a dozen feet, and his right foot came down—hard—on a ledge, while the rope cut deep into the underside of his left bicep. Ended up with a badly sprained ankle and some serious scabbing on his arm. A year later, and his ankle still aches at times.

Was he being cocky? Samuel Taylor doesn't think so.

He hopes not.

He likes to think not. He was aspiring. A calculated risk?

This year a jagged four-inch rock, loosened by his climbing partner's rope, dropped fifty feet and hit Mike on his left foot while he was belaying on a ledge. Puncture wound, bruise. Comes with the territory.

And accidents happen, as they say. To everyone.

Or so does Samuel Taylor conclude, based on his fieldwork.

*

Vick was subletting that summer from a student of Toni Morrison's, Morrison at the time occupying the Schweitzer chair at the New York State Writer's Institute. For a few weeks, Grimm's took him a world away from his language exam (French), his summer graduate course (Arthurian legend), his master's comp (the novel), and Toni Morrison, whom his friend introduced him to briefly one day, and back to a world of summer toil he'd last known as an undergraduate.

But the work at Grimm's was having an unanticipated effect: after his first week on the job, his voice was getting gravelly, and at the end of each day, he was beginning to cough up gobs of thick sputum. He'd always had respiratory issues—asthma, bronchitis. It never occurred to him that he might, in effect, be allergic to work. *Never mind, just get on with it. Need the work.*

One afternoon Manny needs Vick to give him a hand moving some round Sonotube—concrete forms made of a sturdy paper fiber, each ten to twelve feet in length and anywhere from a foot to eighteen inches in diameter. Manny's plan is to hoist himself up on the top rack, where the Sonotube is shelved, and carefully drop each tube seven or eight feet into Vick's waiting hands. Trouble is, the building is dimly lit, and especially dark in this corner where they work. They manage seven or eight drops when one of the tubes catches the edge of the rack and misses Vick's hands, smacking him square in face. He's been wearing his glasses at Grimm's, not his contacts, owing to the incredible amount of dust generated by the work they do. So when it hits, the Sonotube jams his glasses into his face.

He takes his glasses off and feels something above his right eye. He wipes the back of his hand over it. Comes back wet, a dark wet that he sees when he puts his glasses back on.

You all right?

I don't know.

Manny has already scrambled down to have a look for himself. Vick takes his glasses off again and Manny places his large thumb and forefinger over his eye, pulling up his eyebrow.

I think you're gonna need some stitches.

Shit.

Let's walk over to the office. Maybe someone can give you a drive.

Vick takes out his hanky and places it over his eyebrow, soaking up the blood. They walk together to the office building and Vick waits while Manny disappears into one of the interior offices. To judge by the looks on their faces, the staff now endures Vick's presence less with disdain and indifference than with disgust. Manny comes back trailing an anemic, tall man wearing a shirt and tie.

You do know that we're not legally responsible for your injuries.

Yeah—I know. I just need a ride to the hospital. All's I've got is my bike.

Shirt-and-tie turns to Manny.

I think we can have Jack drive him in the van.

Manny nods.

Vick, you take care of yourself. See you tomorrow if you're up to it.

OK, thanks Manny.

Vick waits a few minutes until a small nervous guy emerges. He tells Vick to wait out front while he gets the van. Vick tells him he'll wheel his bike over.

Vick loads the bike into the van, and the two men drive the two miles to the emergency hospital. They don't talk much. Vick keeps sopping up the blood in his hanky. Doesn't want to let up.

When they get to the hospital Vick unloads his bike and places it out of the way, near some bushes. He thanks small nervous guy, and walks in.

It isn't long before he's being attended to by a nurse, who asks him what happened. He needs a tetanus shot. The doctor walks in, stitches him up. Five stitches. The nurse bandages him. As he doesn't have any health insurance, and is not yet a member of the union, all he has is workers' comp. He asks the nurse whether he should plan to go into work the next day—he doesn't want to make things worse.

Sure. Why not? Can't hurt to be active.

He tries to explain that it's tough, dirty, physical work—that he has to pick up heavy stuff, and lug it around, and that even talking with her he can feel the stitches on his face pull. Not to mention the one-inch thick bandage that she's wadded and taped over the top of his right eye, which makes it difficult for him to as much as blink.

We have to lift patients every day and move them from gurney to bed to gurney. Do you know how much patients weigh? This is physical work too, you better believe it.

He didn't come here for another wrestling match. By way of not polarizing things further, he tries to give the nurse to understand that, in this case, work might do more harm than good.

No go.

He concludes that there's no arguing with this silly, stupid bitch, so as soon as she's through, he puts his shirt back on, checks out of the hospital and, feeling a bit woozy, walks his bike the two miles back to his apartment, thinking that right about now he could do with a blowjob or two.

*

There's risk entailed in cranking open discourse.

The computer folks who spend their twelve-hour days dealing with spam and hackers and the like understand the benefits of control, and the hazards of giving it up—of giving up too much control. Viruses, worms—*malicious code*, they call it these days. Best to keep malicious code out of your operating system. Best to use a prophylactic.

But you cannot keep malicious code out of human discourse, social discourse. And if you don't attend to it directly, it'll come in the back door to bite you in the ass.

Or so does Samuel Taylor conclude, based on his fieldwork.

*

Several weeks before taking the job at Grimm's, Vick had split up with his girlfriend of three years—an entirely amicable split, as they'd both known it was over for some time. He started dating a cute—extraordinarily cute—blonde who'd invite him over to her apartment to suck him off in her and her boyfriend's bedroom. That was Round 1. Owing to her regrettable capacity for drink, a habit that would lead to their splitting up, it was difficult to know where Round 2 might lead. He was inside her once for ten minutes, condomless, feeling things were just a bit too tight, when she suddenly realized she'd left her tampon in. Took them a while to get that baby out of there.

Not his proudest engagement, no, but he didn't much give a fuck. He rationalized his behavior by imagining it to be a desperate time, and having been through actual desperate times, he recognized the need for compromising, if not compensating, measures. In light of how hard and how often and how many different ways he came in her, it wouldn't be fair to call Tiffany a compromise. Call their relationship an informed choice, a calculated risk. Call it what you will, his newfound unsafe-ness was exactly what the doctor ordered, and it wasn't long before he was juggling Tiff with two other women. She was doing some juggling herself.

At any rate, he knew his time at Grimm's was coming to an end, since he could feel the buildup in his chest reaching a turning point, a heaviness all too familiar to modern-day lungers. He had a line, too, on a higher-paying job at the university library as Conservation and Preservation Clerk, a ten-dollar title that might, he thought, be of use in compiling his nascent, a-little-bit-late-in-life CV.

The Thursday before what was to be his final day at Grimm's— Friday he finally developed a fever, chills, left work early to see a doctor, started taking antibiotics, and got a call saying he'd landed the library job—this was the weekend of his thirty-first birthday, the same year the city was celebrating its tricentennial—he had already planned a birthday party for himself that Saturday, and invited his grad school friends, two of whom, Jody and Nancy, stayed until the wee hours of the morning to help him clean up the apartment—from which apartment he would bike occasionally over to Krum Kill Road, and do the twenty-mile uphill-downhill loop that includes some nice vistas of the city and surrounds—his brother driving his Yamaha in from Syracuse that Sunday to see him—that final Thursday at Grimm's— which is located a couple of miles down the road from the eastern border of Pine Bush, the sand-duned 58,000-acre pine barrens, the largest in the US, all but 5800 acres of which is now developed, home to the rare Karner Blue butterfly and many other wildlife, including coyotes, and which Melville mentions in *Moby-Dick*, a book he composed while living in Pittsfield, Massachusetts, about forty miles east of Grimm's—that Thursday, around four o'clock, residential customers lined up in the lot to make the day's last run for bricks and cement and whatnot, as they typically did around four o'clock. Usually, one or more of Manny's men would load their vehicles with whatever they purchased from the shirt-and-ties, who stood outside the office handling orders.

This particular Thursday at four o'clock is proving to be an especially busy day for customers, so Manny has them all knock off early to take turns loading cars. All but Lester, who's out sick. They stand together at the storage building entrance, ogling the customers and grunting among themselves the stock sexist observations whenever an attractive woman steps out of her car. Nothing Vick hasn't heard before.

When each transaction is complete, shirt-and-tie waves the receipt at Manny, his cue to have one of the men head down and load the car. Naturally, some conversational energy is also expended in landing upon the best word with which they might denigrate the salesman each time he waves a receipt, and then employing that word among themselves each time he does so.

Pussy.

Vick takes it all in stride—he appreciates a nice ass as much as the next guy, but he's never been too fond of detailing publicly his sexual desires and exploits. That would have to wait some years, until writing provided him with the appropriate, annotated distance. Anyway, it's all standard masculine fare, nothing Vick hasn't heard before.

In the lot pulls a blue Chrysler wagon. The woman gets out—fifties, straight black hair, trim body, nice skirt and blouse. Smiling, very pleasant from this distance. Manny looks at Marty, nodding in the direction of the woman.

Will you get a load of that?

Marty smirks.

Yeah.

Je-sus Christ, what the fuck do we have here?

Manny's demeanor takes Vick completely by surprise. He's never seen Manny get this riled—hot under the collar maybe, but not riled like this. Surprised or no, Vick can see what's coming next, and he wants to be someplace else.

Taking an exam. Reading a novel.

Manny is absolutely fixated on the woman now, and he speaks without taking his eyes off her.

Je-sus Christ. Marty, will you look at this?

Vick turns to look at Marty, who's staring at the woman, then at Robert. Robert rolls his eyes. Vick looks back at Marty.

Retard, you see this shit?

I see it, Marty.

You like it?

Don't think so.

Manny looks at me.

Vick, what do you make of this shit, huh?

Make of what, Manny?

This nigger cunt.

Vick looks away, shrugging.

Marty, get a load of that bitch, will you.

Yeah.

The cunt on that bitch.

Yeah. Fucking cunt.

The salesman waves the receipt. The woman turns, looking up at the men, smiling. Manny and Marty smile back. Vick looks away.

Marty, why don't you go down and give that nigger cunt a hand.

They both laugh.

Sure thing, Pop.

Last Night's Linguine alla Vittorio

Not a sauce, exactly. You'll need 3 or 4 pounds of fresh tomatoes—different varieties, red and yellow would be nice—and a half quart of pearl tomatoes and fresh basil for garnish. Plus one onion (red if you prefer), one small (hot or red bell) pepper. Split the tomatoes in half, quarter the onion, chop the pepper. Arrange in a baking dish with an onion quarter in each corner. Season generously with salt and pepper and Herbes de Provence, drizzle with olive oil, dot the tomatoes with as much as a half stick of butter sliced into ½ tablespoon pads. Add ½ cup of white wine if you like. Bake at 375 degrees for 15-20 minutes covered, then 15-20 minutes uncovered. You want the tomatoes somewhat mushy, with lots of broth. Separate the tomatoes from the broth, placing the broth in a large sauté pan and keeping everything warm.

Boil a pound of linguini (spaghetti will work too) until it's a minute or two from done. Drain and finish in the broth, which should now be boiling. Plate each dish by spooning a few tomatoes over 3 or 4 ounces of spaghetti, adding some broth, and garnishing with a half dozen pearl tomatoes and a sprinkling of chopped basil. Serve with grated Locatelli or Parmigiano-Reggiano, a good loaf of bread, a good glass of red or white. (Be sure to provide your guests with a spoon for any residual broth.) Follow either with a fruit-based salad (strawberries and balsamic works) or with a fresh green salad—nothing fancy, just light oil and vinegar dressing.

Tomorrow Night's Penne alla Kassia

Keep this one simple—try to resist the temptation to embellish (though escarole can be a nice addition). Open a 15 oz can of cannellini, dump the beans into a colander, rinse well under cold water, set aside. Sauté for a minute or so two medium-sized cloves of garlic, minced, in maybe ½ cup of good olive oil. If you like, toss in a few sprinkles of red pepper flakes. Add the cannellini, a teaspoon of salt, two pinches each of thyme, fresh parsley and basil (if you like), and a twist or two of freshly ground black pepper. Stir, let ingredients sauté together for a minute or so, flattening the beans down a bit with back of spoon. Add 1 cup of a dry white wine. Boil off the alcohol—perhaps two or three minutes longer. Add a dollop of butter if you like things creamy. Meanwhile you've been boiling the macaroni, right? Cook the 12 oz of penne to al dente or thereabouts, drain well and toss with the beans, finishing the penne in the beans—maybe one minute more. Add a little olive oil as necessary to keep things winking, or if you prefer, you can add a tablespoon or two of the pasta cooking water. (Chicken broth works too, but that's an embellishment.) Sprinkle with fresh parsley, serve with plenty of grated Locatelli Romano, a good loaf of bread, a good glass of red or white. Follow with a fresh green salad—nothing fancy, just a light oil and vinegar dressing.

Next time you make the dish, adjust seasonings according to taste. For a heartier meal, you can fry up some Italian sausage, adding the beans after the sausage is browned. You can add some onions and tomatoes too, or leftover sauce, to create a sauce for the beans and sausage, but now the recipe begins to look a whole lot like Cannellini alla Catania—and that's a whole nother can of beans. Just remember, like the song says,

"Don't be a fool, eat pasta fazool."

7   LAST NIGHT, AT 5:01 P.M.

Nature is trying very hard to make us succeed, but nature does not depend on us. We are not the only experiment.

R. Buckminster Fuller

Last night, at 5:01 p.m., as he began reading, Samuel Taylor's voice trailed off to a dim buzz, preoccupied as he was with the events of the week prior, when he had let the last of his passwords expire. There would continue to be accounts, but there would be no accounting, for getting and spending had done less to erode his confidence in his fellows than had the actuarial zeal with which they reckoned their successes and failures. Had he the authority, he would call a moratorium on the era's penchant for itemizing every single expenditure, whether of time, money, or energy, as if these were indicative of a person's, or a nation's, or a planet's, emotional or spiritual maturity. The objective, more prudent than it was Protestant, ought to have been the pursuit of something greater than material gain or instant gratification, and aside from the basic arithmetic associated with living within one's means, the only calculation that mattered, he thought, was the one that showed whether the primate who talks the talk but doesn't always walk the walk was individually and collectively happier, healthier, and wiser. And nobody seemed to know how to do *that* math.

Last night, at 5:01 p.m., yet here too was a form of accounting, if one that left decidedly unclear the question of how the burgeoning species was to progress—or at least, to oversee its generational successions—without those endless flows of information captured and rendered as the raw data of statistics, logistics, demographics, the sum total of which had been used to inculcate even the culturally astute in that specious tit-for-tat worldview whereby one could hardly proceed with _____ without assurances that _____ would result. As if there weren't things that one did just because there are some things that one just does, along with things that one just doesn't do. "You see, in this world, there is one awful thing," as Renoir had put it, playing Octave in *The Rules of the Game*, "and that is that everyone has their reasons." His peers had contrived to make spreadsheets of their reasons, awful spreadsheets by which to live their awfully tabulated lives. Samuel Taylor would have none of it.

Last night, at 5:01 p.m., the buzz grew a bit louder, a phoneme or two poking through the sonic haze. So *his* bandwidth, anyway, was to grow narrower momentarily, in anticipation of that still narrower bandwidth that awaited him at trail's end, and which was no longer a remote prospect. He would unplug, in preparation for being unplugged. In which regard, there was much left to do.

Last night, at 5:02 p.m., still: before he could proceed further, he felt he owed himself one last, desperate appeal to that very institution courtesy of which he had developed this stylized rebuttal to the dictates of lifestyle, and with regard to which he had grown, despite his persistent denials to his few confidants, so disaffected. It was no small irony that he hoped to plug into this institution fully—as measured by a professionally respectable wage, in a respectably professional environs—his subsequent and gradual disengagement thus to be accomplished with a modicum of occupational dignity, in the full light of self-actualized day. He was certain that his once and future colleagues would understand. Which is to say, he was certain that they would give not a solitary fuck one way or the other. Such was the nature of the institutional body to which he would make this, his final appeal, and perhaps his final folly.

Last night, at 5:02 p.m., his thoughts drifted to an email he had received from an old friend who still lived in Central New York, who was writing about another old friend in Central New York. No, not "upstate," that reductively expansive appellation with which even newcomers to The City That Never Sleeps were wont to map the rest of the Empire State, as if to distinguish themselves as bona fide urban dwellers bent on establishing the requisite distance between cosmopolis and tree-pocked Appalachian-Adirondack-Finger Laked hinterlands. Central New York was its own region with its own sturdy, regional quirks, and existence there was, on the whole, a half-dozen snow squalls harsher than living in the more temperate, less factory-riven climes of the lower Hudson Valley. Or so his gut reassured him, and in the absence of such indicators as actual days of sunlight and actual unemployment rolls, his gut had proved a reliable arbiter of latitudes and attitudes.

Last night, at 5:03 p.m., upon reading his friend's letter, he had been struck for the first time—and he was genuinely surprised not to have given any thought to this until that moment he'd read the email, just as he was, during *this* moment of recollection, struck again at having been struck so—that he had never himself felt any particular urge to relocate to The City, this despite having lived for so many years within earshot of its orbit, and having for two decades honed his talents as a writer. Why was this? Everyone knows that writers long to gather their apples and oranges, the varied fruits of their literate endeavors, in the Big Apple. The email provided some clues, but he had a few of his own.

Last night, at 5:04 p.m., he had interviewed for a job as a line supervisor—this must have been early in 1977—with Colgate-Palmolive in Jersey City. He'd flown into Newark—his first airline flight, during which his engineer's eye had taken careful note of how a business enterprise built around gravity and its discontents mollified customers in order to mute all but the most unavoidable nuggets of technical or operational gravitas. He tried to imagine himself clutching his seat cushion while bouncing up and down in the currents of the East River. On flights these days, mechanical failure was no less a worry—he'd never entirely gotten over his aerodynamic anxieties—but, like most passengers, the new millennium had delivered other misgivings upon which to cogitate.

Last night, at 5:04 p.m., the Colgate factory was old and dirty, and he'd been unimpressed with the tour past noisy production lines writhing with the motion of toothpaste tubes, and enormous vats saturated with the odor of soap-in-the-making. The Manhattan skyline glistened in the morning and afternoon sun. All he'd known of it first-hand prior to the job interview was a trip with his family to the 1964 World's Fair, and while the Great White Way had gleamed something promisingly artistic to his innocent eyes—he and his brother, as his father's flickering 8mm silents would document, had skipped along the streets of Midtown dressed in knickers—he had yet to grasp how his life might be made to answer to that something. Dinner at an Italian restaurant in Newark later that evening, along with several other candidates, was a blur of small talk and tough eggplant Parmesan. As for the interview, all he would later recall of substance was his final talk with the production manager, in which he expressed his confusion as to why they needed someone with an engineering degree. He'd left the metropolitan area feeling much as if he'd visited the moon, and he knew without knowing it that the moon is a harsh mistress.

Last night, at 5:06 p.m., the buzz grew to a murmur, and the murmur rose to the semblance of a voice, and for an instant Samuel Taylor became aware of his audience, strangers all with the exception of a bright, happy face seated toward the rear of the small auditorium. His eyes caught the eyes of that familiar face, which seemed to wink at him, reminding him of what he was about—and he stuttered. At which, he lifted his gaze to the back wall of the auditorium, regained himself, and continued.

Last night, at 5:08 p.m., he'd learned in the email from his friend that his other friend, whom he had seen only intermittently in recent years, had just been diagnosed with esophageal cancer. The news came as a shock, but he wasn't surprised, and he knew that he was one of a relative handful of friends who could comprehend fully the fact of their friend's illness, and one of the few of that handful who would take the time to comprehend it, both because such comprehension indeed took time and because his livelihood as much as demanded that he take the time. As a writer, he could ill afford to content himself with a nebulous emotional response to mortality. As a writer, he understood the limits of understanding. As a writer, he sought to put things in their proper perspective. As an artist, this meant forsaking any pretense to verisimilitude or ratiocination if the latter interfered with the work of evocation. And as a human being, he knew that his status as writer and artist said nothing as to his capacity for feeling another's pain.

Last night, at 5:09 p.m., to write about a friend who was suffering from a notoriously lethal disease, then, even aside from the matter of survivor guilt, might appear less an act of empathy or generosity than a calculated professional undertaking. And if his conceptual apparatus had a liability, it was this: he could not, for once and for all, square his desire to write with his desire to do good. Having been raised around normative masculinities and femininities that were themselves moored, axiomatically if not always in actuality, to the work ethic of earning what one earned, he had a limited appreciation for those finer amenities one finds lauded among the upper classes. Things, for him, had to have a concrete purpose, and things, for him, included words. It was an easy, if facile, translation, work ethic yielding word ethic.

Last night, at 5:10 p.m., the best he'd been able to muster was to put one desire (writing) into productive conflict with the other (doing good), which meant that the terms of his written articulations, from essay to poem to story, shifted like sand beneath his readers' feet, leaving most feeling much as though they were in the presence of a literate do-gooder with aspirations of someday becoming a good writer. Overweening, in a word.

Last night, at 5:11 p.m., and in which light—here Samuel Taylor struggled to follow his own thoughts, sensing his mouth moving through an especially difficult passage in which the terms *proprioceptive illusion* and *faculty governance* both figured prominently—the Empire City of his ruminations was clearly a foreign habitat, replete as it was with so many messages and messengers, so many of the latter of the sort who took for granted the surplus energies and vocabularies circulating above and below ground. Such concentrations—of people, of customs, of lifeways—could as well inhibit as enhance concentration, unless one had the financial wherewithal to escape for a long walk in the woods. And such assets he never had had, and—here he let his upbringing sneak in a few defeatist licks—likely never would have. His close friends, all but one of whom lived at a considerable distance, would surely understand him, were his close friends to take the time to understand him. His coworkers would never understand him, and he was bemused at their lackluster efforts to do so, which always ended with his being disappointed that the only response he could himself manage was one of bemusement. He would rather fall to his knees, keening, but how to justify doing so when the score for the film based on his colleagues' collective behavior would make ample use of Hungarian Rhapsody No. 2?

Last night, at 5:14 p.m., in short, his friend's email had for the moment emboldened him in his recent determination to disconnect. More guilt, under the circumstances. But if disconnecting *was* the right thing to do, what would come of it in the end was anyone's guess, just as it was anyone's guess whether the enunciation emanating from the podium into the space beyond would effect intention or functionality.

Last night, at 5:16 p.m., a baby cried, one of those grating outbursts that childless listeners deem unforgivable, and Samuel Taylor's eyes once again glimpsed that one familiar face. Would his words have their anticipated effect on this listener at least? He imagined for a moment that she was the only person in attendance. That auditory circuit would benefit, surely, from their having known one another for the better part of a decade, which knowledge had been conditioned by a shared history of loss. She had been there for him when his wife passed away. He had been there for her when her parents were killed.

Last night, at 5:17 p.m., they had been stranded together years before at one of those land-grant installations that dot the country's vast expanses, a place where knowledge is pickled and preserved with such fervor that government funding is typically required to unbottle and distribute it. The two didn't so much seek each other out as flail every limb in that reflex action the body employs when its demise is fast at hand. For him, the semester-by-semester onslaught of memoranda and committee work, coupled with the mindless chit-chat of the school's sterile corridors, had threatened to sap his enthusiasm for the life of the mind. His growing professional anomie had taken a distinctively dire turn when he'd learned, via the grapevine, that tenure was an improbable outcome. For her, owing to a local academic culture that had long been resistant to intellectual work for the sake of the wide-roaming intellect, pursuing a Ph.D. had proved to be as much an exercise in studied negligence—of anything deemed unfashionable, and of any idea that threatened to call the bluff of disciplinary or departmental cohesion—as a labor of love. Somehow, amid all the flailing, they locked arms.

Last night, at 5:18 p.m., and that is all they locked, because he was at the time a happily married man. He'd pledged himself never to engage in another relationship with a student, at any rate, but he was never quite certain he could honor such a pledge without the added incentive of marital fidelity, to which he was, like his wife, utterly committed. They were faculty in the same department—both of them creative writers, his wife adjunct faculty, while he taught on the tenure-track. He'd introduced his wife to the young woman, and both he and his wife made it their mission to show her the doctoral ropes.

Last night, at 5:18 p.m., the three didn't have to work to like one another. They enjoyed that rare form of teacher-student intimacy that can sometimes be engendered by shared interests, similar backgrounds, and a basic affinity of animal natures. The younger woman's friend-mentors gradually metamorphosed into mentor-friends, and they became a sometime social threesome, and occasionally foursome, that fourth wheel as apt to be another woman as another man. As to the alternating sexual partners, the elders chalked it up to youthful experiment, perfectly in step, as they saw it, with 21st-century grad studies in the humanities. For her part, the younger woman confided to the wife that she'd noted a certain queasiness in the older couple's approach to sexual polyvalence, which she chalked up to those mores of a bygone era, progressive at the time, that had doubtless served as the mainstay of their formative years. There might have been flirting all around, but the erotic undertow was held in check by mutual respect.

Last night, at 5:19 p.m., the grapevine bore its customarily bitter fruit: he was denied tenure, even as his wife landed her first tenure-track job a thousand miles east. She negotiated with the new institution to get him adjunct work, which he reluctantly accepted. The three said their goodbyes, and husband and wife trucked off to the prairie where, two years later, tragedy struck. His wife's sudden passing from a heart attack crippled him both emotionally and intellectually. He had only recently begun to see himself clear of the emotional debris that follows a tenure denial—a firing. Now he lost his one and only anchor to the real, and so lost his bearings. Entirely.

Last night, at 5:20 p.m., upon learning of what had transpired, the younger woman hopped a plane immediately, knowing that he would be initially resistant to her intercession, but determined to help him make his way through the various social, legal and familial formalities that circumscribe a person's death. The drive to the graveside service was particularly trying. It was bitterly cold and the two drove together in his old Ford, her few sympathetic overtures counterpointed by his adamantine silence. Yet such trials have a way of ushering us to their aftermaths. A week later, faced with an uncertain professional reception, he was relieved to learn—as was she—that his department chair was supportive, graciously guaranteeing him employment into the foreseeable future. She had her Ph.D. exams to complete, so when it was clear to her that he could function at a minimal level, she left. They hugged at the airport, and she demanded that he post her an email every few days. Sex never entered the picture.

Last night, at 5:21 p.m., she passed her exams "with high honors," completed her dissertation "with distinction," and landed a tenure-track position at a solid second-tier institution on the East Coast. Six months after starting her first academic job, in one of those senseless events that leave survivors forever trying to make sense of things, her parents were killed in a car crash on their way to visit her. Immediately upon hearing the news, he hopped a plane, and lent her the support she had lent him, until it was clear to him that she could function at a minimal level. They hugged at the airport, and he demanded that she post him an email every few days. Sex never entered the picture.

Last night, at 5:22 p.m., a cell phone went off, jolting Samuel Taylor out of his mind's peregrinations. The audience shushed the violator, but Samuel Taylor merely smiled a broad smile and said, "Is that for me?" The crowd erupted in nervous laughter, and as it quieted down, he continued reading, sensing vaguely that the material wasn't going over quite as he'd hoped.

Last night, at 5:22 p.m., on what had he predicated such hope? True, she had encouraged him to make application, both of them believing that he was a good match for the position. And he knew she had worked behind the scenes, discreetly, to improve his chances. But he knew better than most how difficult it would be for a department to hire a man in his fifties, with his history of tenure-track failures. Despite the recent slowdown in his productivity—he insisted on imagining his labor in such terms—he had a substantial publication record, yet this would likely avail him naught given the exigencies of the job market and the preference for young meat at the junior rank. *At the junior rank?* Having spent an inordinate amount of time trimming his grey beard that morning prior to breakfast with the search committee, it occurred to him, for the umpteenth time, that he might be on a fool's errand.

Last night, at 5:22 p.m., and what was hope, after all? The last thing out of Pandora's box. He now scanned the paneled auditorium in which this exchange, if it could yet be called an exchange, was taking place.

He noted, first, the odor of the auditorium, a typically nondescript institutional blend of carpet and seat fabric and wood preservatives, solvents which seem forever to be drying and which, judging by the shape the room was in and the architectural flourishes it boasted, had been giving off vapors only for four or five years. He detected too the faint scent of dogwood wafting in from the outside, the trees in full bloom now. He couldn't tell whether the people who were seated in the room—he counted twenty-three in all, roughly half of whom, to judge by their notepads, looked to be grad students under orders to attend and report—contributed to the odor, which meant that the HVAC system was probably doing its job.

Last night, at 5:22 p.m., next he noticed the quality of the light filtering in through the windowless auditorium, which space, he was told, doubled as a classroom for lecture sections. Glancing at the lighting fixtures, he decided they were all incandescent. A warm light, he thought, if not a very energy-efficient light. From where he was standing, he could just make out the expressions of those seated in the back row, some sixty-odd feet away. And his eyesight wasn't that good.

Last night, at 5:22 p.m., in tactile terms, the room itself was richly textured in browns and ambers and reds, and well maintained. Most inviting, in all, and for those who are alert to such qualities, clear evidence that the campus was doing well financially.

Last night, at 5:22 p.m., the acoustics were astonishingly good. The campus AV expert had helped him test the mike some moments prior to his reading, and even a loud whisper could be heard at every point in the room. Throughout his reading his audience had remained attentively silent, or silently attentive—difficult to know which—and about the only ambient noise he could make out was the syncopated emanation of other bodies breathing, listening.

Last night, at 5:22 p.m., he couldn't taste the room, of course, but he entertained himself with the notion that its flavor resembled paper money.

Last night, at 5:22 p.m., no point in drawing too tight a boundary around the room, for that matter—it wasn't in actuality a closed system, however carefully its confines had been constructed, as the dogwood fragrance confirmed. Electrical energy—for the lights, the mike and speakers, the HVAC system—came from the grid. And in this seaboard state, that meant some combination of coal-fired and nuclear power plants, with a small percentage of natural gas-fired plants and wind power. The lighting was, in truth, a subtle political statement, especially as it was abundantly evident that whoever had designed this room had, from a strictly technical perspective, done his homework. From a strictly technical perspective.

Last night, at 5:22 p.m., did these sense perceptions, at this moment, speak even remotely to the necessary and sufficient conditions for hope? Tough to say. Maybe. No.

Last night, at 5:22 p.m., maybe. He had known hope even after his wife had died. Standing beside her steel casket, he had pressed his palm against the 18-gauge steel. After a few moments, the warmth from his hand made the steel warmer to the touch. When he pulled his hand away, the steel cooled in a few seconds. He tried this several times, and each time he found himself hoping that the steel would warm, for if the steel could warm, so too could his wife's remains, however minutely, and he took comfort in imagining this exchange from life to former life. He liked to think that they had both formed something of an autonomous system, an arbitrary (they both knew there were other fish in the ocean) if motivated (they had chosen to be together) union that, much as life itself swims upstream against the cosmic tide, bucked the institutional surrounds that buttered their bread in order to leave things better than they had found them. Now, with one of them gone, he was viscerally shaken by the age-old insight that even two people joined at the hip can do little to alter life's entropic flows, that their metabolisms would bring them both to the same environmental end, and that this manual transference of energy from flesh and blood through steel to flesh would only feed the earthly compost.

Last night, give me that old-time physics of experimental evidence and conjecture. Last night, fuck string theory. Last night, all the dark matter and dark energy in the world couldn't explain things. Last night, the inertia of flesh.

Last night, at 5:22 p.m., and yet there persisted, as if from nowhere, hope—hope that the steel would warm, which would in turn somehow transmit this warmth. This despite his positive knowledge, as he had it, that the steel *would* warm, that it *would* transmit such warmth. To be hopeful in this context seemed tantamount to ignoring what he knew to be the case. But perhaps he had defined "the case" too narrowly. Perhaps…perhaps hope arose, he thought then, in a special kind of belief, even a faith—faith not as evidence of things unseen, exactly, but as evidence of our desire to make meaningful change, to make change meaningful. In this case, he'd imagined his proximity to her casket, through the mechanism of touch, as bringing her death closer to his life. To have hoped for as much, then, was not to ignore his knowledge of physics new or old, but to enhance it.

Last night, at 5:22 p.m., even understood as the physical representation of countless intentions, the auditorium, taken by itself, was hope-less. In environmental terms, it exerted a powerful effect. But it could not, by its architectural example, offer any lasting solace to the living. It was up to its occupants, he felt, to transform it into a place of hope, a hopeful place. And for this to happen, its occupants had to do more than merely occupy the space—they had truly to inhabit it together, which required, if the space were to be emotionally sustainable, that they believe in one another's capacity for believing in one another. The hard work of attention simply wasn't sufficient. One could attentively believe, disbelieve, accept, reject, identify, discriminate, escape, withdraw. But attention alone, however participatory or individuating, was not the stuff of belief; attention might heighten awareness, might presage knowledge, but it could not instill hope. Attention was primarily a critical faculty, whereas hope presumed belief of an order preempting attention, preempting even the conscious act of believing.

Last night, at 5:22 p.m., once he had found himself inquiring into the nature of this belief, this faith, he saw that it had been there right along. He felt that everyone had access to it, that it was probably anthropological, certainly cultural, and for those so inclined, possibly divine in nature. But he had no idea what it was, precisely, that activated hope, or why, for some, activation seemed nigh impossible; though here again he suspected that, like energy itself, hope ought to be construed as an open system within the human-to-human orbit. If it could not offset exchanges of entropy, hope replenished nonetheless, and—Pope was right—was replenished. And if not forever and ever, at least for as long as a single sentient biped could feel.

Last night, at 5:22 p.m., he had a hunch, too, that hope might be a precondition for forgiveness, for the most difficult act of forgiveness, in his secularist outlook, was to forgive those for whom there is no hope. Social abominations. Yes, to abandon all hope was to enter some kind of hell. One must hope against hope, however vague such hope might be.

Last night, at 5:22 p.m., all of which various and sundry stipulations held for that reader—better, performer—whose job it was not simply to make available, or to make accessible, or to make inviting, but to make absolutely indispensable. A root act.

Last night, at 5:22 p.m., but this wasn't a church, and he wasn't giving the Sermon on the Mount. This wasn't a panel presentation either. This was a job talk. *A job talk.* The slightest blunder or blindness would be fodder for the search committee. One ought to be trenchant, but never mordant. Demanding, but never difficult. Enthusiastic, but never fervent.

Last night, at 5:23 p.m., and without quite understanding why, Samuel Taylor suddenly became angry. He looked out over the auditorium. Who were these people to sit in judgment of him? And were they in fact sitting in judgment, or was this all but a charade put on to appease a new hire by making it appear as if her former teacher really was a serious candidate for the position? He'd seen such antics before, and was keenly aware of how the academic aversion to confrontation often led to the most indirect inquiries, wasteful requisitions, and procedurally arcane practices. Steely-eyed, he scanned each member of his audience, and in each countenance and posture, he now discerned some small quotient of indifference, even skepticism. They were looking at him askance, he was certain of it. And he grew angrier still, his face flushing perceptibly as he continued, his intonations rising one or two decibels higher.

*

Last night, at 5:01 p.m., Samuel Taylor could not have known it at the time, nor would he have wanted to discuss it in such terms had he been made aware of it, but there was no end of reasons for his anger, the upshot of which was the nagging feeling that to unplug was a petty and unwarranted tactic—a cop-out.

Last night, at 5:01 p.m., however conspicuous his anger might have been to others who knew him, Samuel Taylor had had little sense himself of how much rage had infiltrated his everyday being. Sure, he knew he walked around pissed off half the time, but that wasn't the half of it. Had he been sensitive to his predicament, more emotionally introspective or accessible, he would have intuited that he was angry, first, with himself, here on this prospective campus, for having gotten his hopes up, and once having done so, for having acquitted himself with such manifest confidence.

Last night, at 5:01 p.m., he was angry, next, with his young ally, for having conspired, albeit with the best of intentions, to bring him to this performative denouement.

Last night, at 5:01 p.m., he was angry with his faculty audience for feigning interest, and angry with his student audience, for not feigning interest.

Last night, at 5:01 p.m., he was angry at the school that hosted him, and at academe generally, for sanctioning such dog and pony shows.

Last night, at 5:01 p.m., and yet his anger was far more comprehensive than any *in situ* litany might suggest. He was angry with his fellow teachers for putting a good face on intolerable working conditions. He was angry with his fellow writers for letting aesthetics obscure their publishing ambitions. He was angry with politicians for acting as hypocritically as the average Joe. He was angry with lobbyists for being lobbyists. He was angry with physicians for failing to be healers. He was angry with lawyers for failing to do justice. He was angry with men and women of the cloth for their doctrinaire approach to human misery, and with judges for neglecting to judge themselves. He was angry with news anchors for failing to report the most urgent news. He was angry with workers for not showing up to work. He was angry with entrepreneurs for advocating such narrowly entrepreneurial agenda, and he was angry with CEOs for thinking they deserve a place in heaven. He was angry with fiction writers for avoiding poetry, he was angry with poets for their patrician sensibilities, and he was angry with Ezra Pound for being Ezra Pound. He was angry with creationists for taking too much on faith, with scientists for avoiding the issue of faith, with artists for avoiding the findings of science, with citizens for their ignorance of art. He was angry with soldiers for not boning up on the relevant history, and with historians for knowing so little about the dangers of reconnaissance. He was angry with landlords for being such jerks, and with tenants for not living up to their end of the bargain. He was angry with men for being insufficiently local, with women for being insufficiently global, with humanists for being insufficiently humble, with intellectuals for being insufficiently creative, with the left and with the right for being insufficiently generous. He was angry with his friends for not cherishing their friendship, and with his family for wasting time on bickering. He was angry with mediocre thinkers, mediocre cooks, mediocre drivers, and mediocre actors. He was angry with people and their pets. He was angry with amateurs for thinking they were professionals, and with professionals for behaving like amateurs. He was angry with musicians and professional athletes and just about everyone he knew at one time or another, including himself, for falling under the sway of drugs, and he was angry at puritanical attitudes toward drugs. He was angry at public discourse for being so silly, and at private discourse for being so dumb. He was angry with adults both for acting like children and for treating children like adults. He was angry with pro-lifers for thinking they can control what women do with their bodies, and at the gun lobby for thinking that gun control is a violation of personal liberty. He was angry with pro-choicers for quibbling over the point at which life begins, and with gun control advocates for taking their disgust with firearms too far. He was angry with those who overstated the threat of terrorism for their own ideological ends, and he was angry with those who understated the threat of terrorism for their own ideological ends, and he was angry with terrorists for putting human life at the mercy of ideological ends. He was angry at the entire spectrum of misapprehensions and misdeeds surrounding the word *immigration*, and he was angry at how the words *neoliberal* and *privatization* invariably pointed the general public in the wrong directions. He was angry at the Taft-Hartley Act, he was angry at the selling of public infrastructure to private interests, he was angry with those activists who alleged "there's no difference between Democrats and Republicans," and he was angry with Democrats for being so much like Republicans. He was angry at airports and airlines, the Interstate Highway System, cruise ships, and ecotourism. He was angry with those who thought they could postpone indefinitely the ravages of age, and he was angry at entropy. He was angry at supermarket chains for treating produce like hand-me-downs, at US automakers for fighting every attempt to raise gas mileage standards, at the oil industry for its sheer greed, at the biofuel industry for hawking one or two *really* bad ideas, and at the publishing conglomerates for publishing so much tripe. He was angry at the marketplace for marketing shit, at the electorate for not knowing shit from Shinola, at the public relations industry for making shit up. And he was angry at any number of government agencies and public institutions for making such a mockery of government agencies and public institutions, and doing so with such predictable shamelessness.

Last night, at 5:01 p.m., he might have been angry, too, for not having found it within himself, the night before, to fuck the woman he and his wife had both coached through her doctorate, who was now his strongest advocate and confidante. She had wanted to fuck him, she had said so in the hotel lobby. She had used the word *fuck* in fact, and it fell from her lips like manna to this angry older man. He could hardly restrain himself, but he knew that the guilt that would invariably ensue would cause him only more grief. And so his very conscience angered him.

Last night, at 5:01 p.m., but what angered him most was finding himself alone in middle age. Yes, he was angry with his wife, you bet your sweet ass he was—angry with her for not being stronger than she was. He knew this was wrong, of course. He knew he should have reserved *that* anger for the industrial-financial empire that was busy poisoning all of creation with processes and products that humankind nonetheless could ill afford to do without, to which processes and products most who knew her felt her asthmatic self had ultimately succumbed. But he just couldn't help himself, his proclivity for concretizing leading him to assign some modicum of blame to the primary embodiment of the unfolding tragedy: the victim, his one and only, Nora. Nora, who'd worked too hard, too long, under such obvious respiratory duress. He had wanted only, as the song went, to string along with Nora. *To string along.* Nora's death left him with a modest insurance payout, three novels to be edited posthumously, and a life beyond repair. Blaming Nora made him even angrier with himself, anger escalating, as is its wont, into even greater anger, until he was angry at being angry. If anger had become his tacit raison d'être, an article of unspoken faith, it was no less for that uncontainable. And this he could not see.

Last night, at 5:01 p.m., and so he was one angry man, and with few exceptions—the anger directed at his wife, and his unbridled contempt for class entitlement, a target he couldn't resist—it was fair to say that he came by it honestly, at least. At least he had good reason to be sad, hurt, fearful of losing those few laurels on which he had never rested, and which had only briefly earned him a measure of professional respect and security. He wasn't the first angry man, and he wouldn't be the last, but he was one goddamn good and angry son of a bitch of a man. He used to be an angry young man, and he was on his way to becoming an angry old man, and while he knew deep down inside that his occasional flares of anger were unbecoming, and that they might signal a core imbalance, an imbalance that might kill him before his time, he knew also that anger in general suited his personality in ways that it didn't suit everyone's—a salesman's, for instance, or a funeral director's—and so he, or rather, his unconscious self had made a volatile peace with his angry temperament. He rarely lost any sleep over it, which he took as a sure sign that it couldn't be doing him any lasting harm. His wife had pleaded with him to do something about his anger, but he'd refused, believing that it was the only thing keeping him in the game, fighting the good fight, the periodic social indiscretion aside. He might have been right, and she might have been right, and they both might have been right. But it wasn't doing his wife any good, that much was clear. And he was, in truth, too self-conscious—though he flattered himself with the thought that he was less self-conscious than self-aware—not to recognize his failure to put his anger to more serviceable ends. Incapable of entirely grasping his predicament, then, something in the back of his brain nonetheless told him that unplugging could be seen, and would be seen, as but an angry reaction to such failure, hence an extension of it. And so it nagged at him.

*

Last night, at 5:23 p.m., he made a conscious decision now to raise his voice another decibel or two, and as the amplified volume again trailed off to a dim buzz, he revisited any number of past occupations for which a raised voice was less an act of aggression than a handy social tool. Take pick and shovel work, for instance, or its equivalent, of which backbreaking activities he had managed only a few months over the course of his entire life, and which was nowhere to be found on his vita. You needed to grow some balls fast in those quarters, he thought, and he knew he'd profited from balls grown in such quarters to the extent that nobody, as in *nobody*, had dared to push him around professionally—to his face, anyway. It was a nice corrective, too, to the glorification of manual labor to which many of his male students and a few social theorists, altogether too twee, seemed prone. He would remind them that digging a ditch at minimum wage is one thing, and digging a ditch at minimum wage under the ruthless eye of a slave driver quite another. And he knew, as well, that the calluses he'd boasted on his young palms, and the general level of fitness he'd maintained into middle age, had exempted him from despairing, like some of this colleagues, that intellectual work was a refined form of alienated labor. He'd managed to soldier on, and without the benefit of military service. So while his may have been alienated labor, certainly—how, given his predicament, might it not have been?—he would never be alienated from the joy he took in the work of writing and, intermittently, teaching.

Last night, at 5:24 p.m., plant engineering, as he'd known it anyway, was another venue ripe for the occasional throat clearing. You'd have a rough go of it trying to negotiate the hourly-salary job site without a firm handshake and a fuck-you-too temperament. But what the hell—pussyfooting around one's coworkers wasn't the way to go about building camaraderie anyway. Granted, he was predisposed toward a Hawksian notion of men and women—or woman—bonding, but he'd always believed that if you couldn't lay it on the line with someone, you weren't friends anyway. That word, "friends," did far too much work in US culture—as everyone sooner or later discovers—and he had no interest in being collegial for the sake of some rarefied notion of collegiality.

Last night, at 5:25 p.m., with only minutes remaining, Samuel Taylor peered out over his audience, making direct eye contact now with the most withdrawn countenances. The associations kept piling up.

At 5:25 p.m., the scholars he'd known, most of them, had an especially difficult time of appreciating the blue-collar nature of some white-collar work, and how blue-collar values might comprise a nice antidote to white-collar decorum. He'd had a much easier time of it, by and large, with the generation of scholars prior to his own—the men of his father's and mother's generation, so many of whom had served in World War II or Korea, and who owed their advanced degrees to the G.I. Bill. Most of those guys, and there weren't many left, had experienced the leveling effect—of race, class, even sexual orientation—brought about by mutual struggle against a common adversary. They might have been wedded to ideals that seemed a bit quaint in the wake of those sophisticated theories and methods that cropped up in the sixties—and though often sympathetic to the aims of feminism, these men usually found it difficult to deal with women in liberated terms, let alone as equals—but at least they had their feet planted firmly on the ground. There was nothing fey about them—you knew where they were coming from. And the best of them were gentlemen.

Last night, at 5:26 p.m., and as for his own generation, it was a mixed bag. He had no problem with his peers on the basis of their military service or lack thereof. Several among his closest friends had joined one or another branch of the armed forces during that oddly peaceful and somewhat dejected and eventually hedonistic period that marked the end of one era and the beginning of another. He might be more specific, he thought, and zeroed in on the years 1974 to 1978. Yeah, the public mood was different then.

Last night, at 5:26 p.m., he doubted whether one could really speak intelligently of things like "public mood," or whether such terms were merely a way of sidestepping something about which one had not thought rigorously enough. Must one think *rigorously* about everything? he thought. Of what does *rigorous* thought consist? How does one think *rigorously* about mixed bags of experience? Does *rigorous* imply a connect-the-dots approach to the dissemination of knowledge, the instantiation of discourse?

Last night, at 5:26 p.m., *discourse*? More intellectual hoodoo?

Last night, at 5:26 p.m., and what of *dialogue*, that darling of intellectual presumptions in which so many academic events locate their putative purpose? For a moment Samuel Taylor fancied himself a dissenting subterranean, appearing at cave's entrance to stick out his tongue and yell, *Woo hoo!*

Last night, at 5:26 p.m., still: he rebuffed himself, what to do about a flat-earth population oblivious to climate change and indifferent to evolutionary theory?

Last night, at 5:26 p.m., he was stuck, and for the second time that afternoon, Samuel Taylor stuttered. And recovered.

Last night, at 5:26 p.m., OK: what grated on him about his baby boom peers had become a matter largely of class values and revaluations as gauged against the onset of adulthood. In another, less gilded age, he might have concluded that too many had sold their souls for the sake of comfort and security, and he might have left it at that. But in every direction he turned he saw less an engaged struggle with inequities or injustices—or even the elemental and justifiable desire to want to live something like the good life, the life without constant struggle—than a set of affectations purchased at too dear a price. What had kicked the shit out of his cohort in particular, he did not presume to know. And he did not presume to blame his friends per se. Not everyone gets a fair shake, and he tended to ascribe to social theories that correlated a person's stock of fortitude, say, with the effects of socialization. To have viable work options, and viable dreams, was to his way of thinking a matter of character, yes, but character was itself a function of innumerable social and genetic and environmental and, sure, economic factors. Along, of course, with something called *the breaks*. And in an age where *haves* could be energized ontologically by talk of a creative class sharing their wares in a creative commons, it was little wonder that the creative itself could be seen as a means of enabling the entrepreneurial spirit in *haves* and *have-nots* alike. As to the breaks, everyone had equal access to same, right? Onward! Workshops for would-be CEOs, poetry retreats for CEOs: just try to write *that* out of your system, would-be auteur.

Last night, at 5:27 p.m., and him? He'd managed to soldier on, and without the benefit of a trust fund. Or maybe he'd just gotten lucky.

*

Last night, at 5:28 p.m., that was it—that was the moment at which Samuel Taylor realized that he had made a serious miscalculation in opting to read from the current draft of his manuscript, and not because it was a draft. The decision regarding whom to hire—he accepted this with a degree of equanimity the likes of which he had until now thought himself constitutionally incapable—had indeed already been made. He would not get the offer. And he would not get the offer because there was no luck in it for him.

Last night, at 5:28 p.m., there was no luck in it for him. Samuel Taylor could not explain how he knew this to be the case, and he would in later years refer his interlocutors, half-jokingly, to "bad vibes" by way of an explanation. But vibes, he now understood, were precisely the issue, and bad vibes were no joke. Everything he had known and sensed up to this point in his life, coupled with everything he could know and sense of the interview process up to and including the vibes of that prior bit of third-person-limited narration, flooded him with an awareness of just how out of step he was with the situation at hand. It wasn't merely his age, or his track record, or his intellect, or his talent, such as it was. Or his face. He would never be able to drag these people kicking and screaming to some rhetorical phase change. Nothing he could do would win over such an audience, because such an audience was not to be won over. In fact the candidate who was to get the offer eventually—here too Samuel Taylor persuaded himself that this was anything but speculation—would not do so by winning over *anyone.* He or she would get the nod because a constellation of institutional contingencies could be satisfied only by that person, in that place, at that time. All that person had to do was not fall flat on his or her face—using charisma or charm to offset any lingering suspicion, on the part of all parties, that what was sought, finally, was a glorified factotum—and his or her candidacy would be secure. He'd been there, done that. And once the new hire's tenure clock started ticking, a new set of contingencies would take effect, in many cases having only tangentially to do with expertise, achievement, reputation.

Agency would be put to the task of answering to other, less discrete, more esoteric variables. It was a perfectly perfunctory exposition, thus all the more likely to come to pass.

Last night, at 5:29 p.m., in fact, by trying to offer his audience something he thought they wanted to hear, he'd wasted an opportunity to say something they needed to hear, something they would recognize as absolutely necessary once they heard it. A root act. For upwards of thirty minutes, he'd tissued over any number of topical issues with a sly professional allegory. He'd busied himself with demonstrating how the personal and the professional intersect in ways that simply can't be reduced to those tired antagonisms exploited by some to characterize higher education in the first decade of the 21st century. But what he should have been demonstrating instead was just how close the literate species is to entering an era when billions on the planet would be forever relegated to lives of despair and suffering and premature death, and where survival would be doled out on the basis of inheritance—of assets, of genes, of connections. Today was bringing us a tomorrow in which, OK, some lucky millions purchased more and more of less and less—the "long tail" that Chris Anderson had at the time advanced as a new business model—while more and more unlucky millions struggled for less and less.

Last night, at 5:30 p.m., it was clear now: he wasn't risking enough, not nearly enough to do justice to this push-come-to-shove world, to push it past its equilibrium point in order to catalyze a different approach to the living and the dead. Here he was, brandishing some erudite form of shoptalk in which internecine grievances, no matter how devastatingly personal, would likely be deemed trifles absent their connection to scorched-earth policies that had produced a surgically traumatized sphere. Instead of droning on and on about the profession, he should have been addressing the end of the world, the potentially catastrophic consequences of ordinary endeavors. And if he had not a clue as to how to go about doing so without coming off as a crank of the Apocalypse, at least he was no longer conflicted, at least he knew what purpose might be better served at future such events, were there to be, for him, future such events. Either that or one would do well to hold one's peace.

Last night, at 5:31 p.m., he lowered his voice, hearing fully its familiar cadence for the first time during his delivery. He began to feel sorry for himself, for he understood that his thoughts had once again tottered on that slippery divide between good writing and good deeds. Then he thought better of it, wrapped up his reading, and felt a slight burn as he tightened his gut and stuck out his jaw to polite applause, wondering what the Q & A would bring.

MICHAL AJVAZ, *The Golden Age,*
The Other City.

PIERRE ALBERT-BIROT, *Grabinoulor.*

YUZ ALESHKOVSKY, *Kangaroo.*

FELIPE ALFAU, *Chromos.*
Locos.

IVAN ÂNGELO, *The Celebration,*
The Tower of Glass.

ANTÓNIO LOBO ANTUNES,
Knowledge of Hell,
The Splendor of Portugal.

ALAIN MRIAS-MISSON, *Theatre of Incest.*

JOHN ASHBERY AND JAMES SCHUYLER,
A Nest of Ninnies.

ROBERT ASHLEY, *Perfect Lives.*

GABRIELA AVIGUR-ROTEM,
Heatwave and Crazy Birds.

DJUNA BARNES, *Ladies Almanack,*
Ryder.

JOHN BARTH, *Letters,*
Sabbatical.

DONALD BARTHELME, *The King,*
Paradise.

SVETISLAV BASARA, *Chinese Letter.*

MIQUEL BAUÇÀ, *The Siege in the Room.*

RENÉ BELLETTO, *Dying.*

MAREK BIEŃCZYK, *Transparency.*

ANDREI BITOV, *Pushkin House.*

ANDREJ BLATNIK, *You Do Understand.*

LOUIS PAUL BOON, *Chapel Road,*
My Little War,
Summer in Termuren.

ROGER BOYLAN, *Killoyle.*

IGNÁCIO DE LOYOLA Brandão,
Anonymous Celebrity,
Zero.

BONNIE BREMSER, *Troia: Mexican*
Memoirs.

CHRISTINE BROOKE-ROSE,
Amalgamemnon.

BRIGID BROPHY, *In Transit.*

GERALD L. BRUNS,
Modern Poetry and the Idea of Language.

GABRIELLE BURTON, *Heartbreak Hotel.*

MICHEL BUTOR, *Degrees,*
Mobile.

G. CABRERA INFANTE,
Infante's Inferno.
Three Trapped Tigers.

JULIETA CAMPMPOS,
The Fear of Losing Eurydice.

ANNE CARSON, *Eros the Bittersweet.*

ORLY CASTEL-BLOOM, *Dolly City.*

LOUIS-FERDINAND CÉLINE,
Castle to Castle.
Conversations with Professor Y,
London Bridge,
Normance,
North,
Rigadoon.

MARIE CHAIX,
The Laurels of Lake Constance.

HUGO CHARTERIS, *The Tide Is Right.*

ERIC CHEVILLARD, *Demolishing Nisard.*

MARC CHOLODENKO, *Mordechai*
Schamz.

JOSHUA COHEN, *Witz.*

EMILY HOLMES COLEMAN,
The Shutter of Snow.

ROBERT COOVER, *A Night at the Movies.*

STANLEY CRAWFORD, *Log of the S.S,*
The Mrs Unguentine,
Some Instructions to My Wife.

RENÉ CREVEL, PUTTING *My Foot in It.*

RALPH CUSACK, *Cadenza.*

NICHOLAS DELBANCO,
The Count of Concord,
Sherbrookes.

NIGEL DENNIS, *Cards of Identity.*

PETER DIMOCK,
A Short Rhetoric for Leaving the Family.

ARIEL DORFMFMAN, *Konfidenz.*

COLEMAN DOWELL, *Island People,*
Too Much Flesh and Jabez.

ARKADII DRAGOMOSHCHENKO,
Dust.

RIKKI DUCORNET,
The Complete Butcher's Tales,
The Fountains of Neptune,
The Jade Cabinet,
Phosphor in Dreamland.

WILLIAM EASTLAKE, *The Bamboo Bed,*
Castle Keep,
Lyric of the Circle Heart.

JEAN ECHENOZ, *Chopin's Move.*

STANLEY ELKIN, *A Bad Man,*
Criers and Kibitzers, Kibitzers and Criers,
The Dick Gibson Show,
The Franchiser,
The Living End,
Mrs. Ted Bliss.

FRANÇOIS EMMMMANUEL,
Invitation to a Voyage.

SALVADOR ESPRIU,
Ariadne in the Grotesque Labyrinth.

LESLIE A. FIEDLER,
Love and Death in the American Novel.

JUAN FILLOY, *Op Oloop.*

ANDY FITCH, *Pop Poetics.*

GUSTAVE FLAUBERT,
Bouvard and Pécuchet.

KASS FLEISHER, *Talking out of School.*

FORD MADOX FORD,
The March of Literature.

JON FOSSE, *Aliss at the Fire,*
Melancholy.

MAX FRISCH, *I'm Not Stiller,*
Man in the Holocene.

CARLOS FUENTES, *Christopher Unborn,*
Distant Relations,
Terra Nostra,
Where the Air Is Clear.

TAKEHIKO FUKUNAGA,
Flowers of Grass.

WILLIAM GADDIS, J R, *The Recognitions.*

JANICE GALLOWAY, *Foreign Parts,*
The Trick Is to Keep Breathing.

WILLIAM H H. GASS,
Cartesian Sonata and Other Novellas,
Finding a Form,
A Temple of Texts,
The Tunnel,
Willie Masters' Lonesome Wife.

GÉRARD GAVARRY, *Hoppla! 1 2 3.*

ETIENNE GILSON,
The Arts of the Beautiful, Forms
and Substances in the Arts.

C. S S. GISCOMBE, *Giscome Road,*
Here.

DOUGLAS GLOVER,
Bad News of the Heart.

WITOLD GOMBROWICZ,
A Kind of Testament.

PAULO EMÍLIO SALES GOMES,
P's Three Women.

GEORGI GOSPODINOV, *Natural Novel.*

JUAN GOYTISOLO, *Count Julian,*
Juan the Landless,
Makbara,
Marks of Identity.

HENRY GREEN, *Back,*
Blindness,
Concluding,
Doting,
Nothing.

JACK GREEN, *Fire the Bastards!*

JIŘI´ GRUŠA, *The Questionnaire.*

MELA HARTWIG,
Am I a Redundant Human Being?

JOHN HAWKES, *The Passion Artist,*
Whistlejacket.

ELIZABETH HEIGHWAY, ED.,
Contemporary Georgian Fiction.

ALEKSANDAR HEMON, ED.,
Best European Fiction.

FOR A FULL LIST OF PUBLICATIONS, VISIT: www.dalkeyarchive.com

ABDELWAHAB MEDDEB, *Talismano.*

GERHARD MEIER, *Isle of the Dead.*

HERMAN MELVILLE, *The Confidence-Man.*

AMANDA MICHALOPOULOU, *I'd Like.*

STEVEN MILLHAUSER,
The Barnum Museum,
In the Penny Arcade.

RALPH J. MILLS, JR., *Essays on Poetry.*

MOMUS, *The Book of Jokes.*

CHRISTINE MONTALBETTI,
The Origin of Man,
Western.

OLIVE MOORE, *Spleen.*

NICHOLAS MOSLEY, *Accident,*
Assassins,
Catastrophe Practice,
Experience and Religion,
A Garden of Trees,
Hopeful Monsters,
Imago Bird,
Impossible Object,
Inventing God,
Judith,
Look at the Dark,
Natalie Natalia,
Serpent,
Time at War.

WARREN MOTTE, *Fables of the Novel: French*
Fiction since 1990,
Fiction Now: The French Novel in the 21st
Century,
Oulipo: A Primer of Potential Literature.

GERALD MURNANE, *Barley Patch,*
Inland.

YVES NAVARRE,
Our Share of Time,
Sweet Tooth.

DOROTHY NELSON, *In Night's City,*
Tar and Feathers.

ESHKOL NEVO, *Homesick.*

WILFRIDO D D. NOLLEDO,
But for the Lovers.

FLANN O'BRIEN, *At Swim-Two-Birds,*
The Best of Myles,
The Dalkey Archive,
The Hard Life,
The Poor Mouth,
The Third Policeman.

CLAUDE OLLIER, *The Mise-en-Scène,*
Wert and the Life Without End.

GIOVANNI ORELLI, *Walaschek's Dream.*

PATRIK OUŘEDNÍK, *Europeana,*
The Opportune Moment, 1855.

BORIS PAHOR, *Necropolis.*

FERNANDO DEL PASO,
News from the Empire,
Palinuro of Mexico.

ROBERT PINGET, *The Inquisitory,*
Mahu or The Material,
Trio.

MANUEL PUIG, *Betrayed by Rita Hayworth,*
The Buenos Aires Affair,
Heartbreak Tango.

RAYMYMOND QUENEAU, *The Last Days,*
Odile,
Pierrot Mon Ami,
Saint Glinglin.

ANN QUIN, *Berg,*
Passages,
Three,
Tripticks.

ISHMAEL REED, *The Free-Lance Pallbearers,*
The Last Days of Louisiana Red,
Ishmael Reed: The Plays,
Juice!,
Reckless Eyeballing,
The Terrible Threes,
The Terrible Twos,
Yellow Back Radio Broke-Down.

JASIA REICHARDT,
15 Journeys Warsaw to London.

NOËLLE REVAZ,
With the Animals.

JOÃO UBALDO RIBEIRO,
House of the Fortunate Buddhas.

⑤ SELECTED DALKEY ARCHIVE TITLES

▣ SELECTED DALKEY ARCHIVE TITLES

LUCIAN DAN TEODOROVICI,
Our Circus Presents . . .

NIKANOR TERATOLOGEN,
Assisted Living.

STEFAN THEMERSON,
Hobson's Island,
The Mystery of the Sardine,
Tom Harris.

TAEKO TOMIOKA, *Building Waves.*

JOHN TOOMEY, *Sleepwalker.*

JEAN-PHILIPPPPE TOUSSAINT,
The Bathroom,
Camera,
Monsieur,
Reticence,
Running Away,
Self-Portrait Abroad,
Television,
The Truth about Marie.

DUMITRU TSEPENEAG,
Hotel Europa,
The Necessary Marriage,
Pigeon Post,
Vain Art of the Fugue.

ESTHER TUSQUETS,
Stranded.

DUBRAVKA UGRESIC,
Lend Me Your Character,
Thank You for Not Reading.

TOR ULVEN, *Replacement.*

MATI UNT,
Brecht at Night,
Diary of a Blood Donor,
Things in the Night.

ÁLVARO URIBE AND OLIVIA SEARS, EDS.,
Best of Contemporary Mexican Fiction.

ELOY URROZ, *Friction,*
The Obstacles.

LUISA VALENZUELA,
Dark Desires and the Others,
He Who Searches.

PAUL VERHAEGHEN,
Omega Minor.

AGLAJA VETERANYI,
Why the Child Is Cooking in the Polenta.

BORIS VIAN, *Heartsnatcher.*

LLORENÇ VILLALONGA, *The Dolls' Room.*

TOOMAS VINT, *An Unending Landscape.*

ORNELA VORPSI,
The Country Where No One Ever Dies.

AUSTRYN WAINHOUSE,
Hedyphagetica.

CURTIS WHITE,
America's Magic Mountain,
The Idea of Home,
Memories of My Father Watching TV,
Requiem.

DIANE WILLIAMS,
Excitability: Selected Stories, Romancer Erector.

DOUGLAS WOOLF,
Wall to Wall,
Ya! & John-Juan.

JAY WRIGHT,
Polynomials and Pollen,
The Presentable Art of Reading Absence.

PHILIP WYLIE, *Generation of Vipers.*

MARGUERITE YOUNG,
Angel in the Forest,
Miss MacIntosh, My Darling.

REYOUNG, *Unbabbling.*

VLADO ŽABOT, *The Succubus.*

ZORAN ŽIVKOVIĆ, *Hidden Camera.*

LOUIS ZUKOFSKY, *Collected Fiction.*

VITOMIL ZUPAN, *Minuet for Guitar.*

SCOTT ZWIREN, *God Head.*

FOR A FULL LIST OF PUBLICATIONS, VISIT: www.dalkeyarchive.com